Westport - The Nine to Set Out

A journey from Bridport to Westport

Horst D. Lindenau

Amazon books 2020

ISBN: 9781086623062
Disclaimer

Although the author of this pamphlet has taken great care to ensure the authenticity of the information published herein, we are not responsible, in whole or in part, for any consequences which may occur to the reader by following any instructions, ideas and descriptions given in this book. We also do not guarantee that the places and events described within here will be the same or similar as they described.

It is essential that the reader who visits any of the described places should seek medical advice to ensure he/she is fit to do so and understands the risks. Information and recommendations presented in this book are based on own personal experience and extensive research. Application of the recommendations and information given in this book are undertaken at the individuals own risk. All recommendations and information given here are without any guarantee on the part of the author or publisher, their agents or employees. Of necessity, the author and publisher disclaim all liability in connection with the use of information presented herein, which should always be used on a basis of a gift – sound common sense.

Note: Throughout the book individuals are referred to as "he". This should, of course, be taken to mean "he" or "she" or "any other" where appropriate.

Preface

This book of a few words and many images is a practical and valuable source of information if one likes to travel to the beautiful town of Westport in the Republic of Ireland. A source for the one who wants to travel a while with a group of friends and not only escape the daily trot but find joy and fun. A helpful hand for those who like a pint of Guinness and sometimes strong language but clear speech and common sense.

Eh, what am I talking about? This book is the diary of a trip from the little town of Bridport in the southwest of England to the little town of Westport at the northern west coast of Ireland which happened in May 2019.

This trip was the tenth of its kind initialised and organized mainly by Mr. Ivan St Pierre who lives today in Bridport but is of Irish origin. As Ivan knows this much of his beloved emerald island, he started to encourage friends of his in Bridport to travel there together and enjoy a few days of fun and leisure shared with the right people.

And there is no better place in Ireland to do so than in Westport in county Mayo right at the wild Atlantic. Westport was rated by the Irish Times once as the best place to live in Ireland. Of course, that will attract visitors from all over the world. Westport is famous among the Americans with Irish heritage roots, they come in thousands each year and this is very easily done since the connection via nearby Knock airport was established. Many German tourists are seen in town too. For them Ireland and especially nearby Achill is famous. And there are the odd numbers flying in from the UK like us.

Ireland might be a small island, but with a big heart. Ireland is a world unto itself, rolling green hills, with an astonishing coastline and with plenty of vibrant towns and villages. And one thing I can say already: with very friendly people!

Some men from Bridport assembled first in groups of four or sometimes five guys and spent each year a week or so over in Westport. Early days my good friend Chinner was on board and as he knows I had lived a year myself in Ireland before and love the folks there, he tried since then to encourage me and join in. "No way"! I thought I can't stand firstly a trip with several men, always hated group travelling and honest; I couldn't bare the idea of eight days drinking either!

How wrong was I?

Finally, I joined, and it was one of my best holidays ever. I enjoyed great company and friendship, a great place to investigate and ever so good to be back in Ireland again. Read on and judge yourself. By the way… they go again.

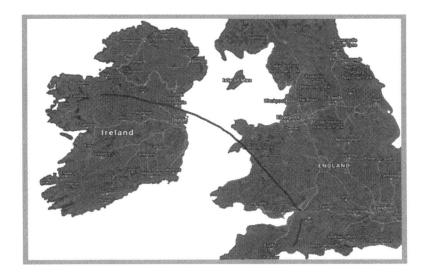

Our journey from Bridport in our own cars to Bristol and flight to Knock airport with Ryan Air and proceed by hired cars to Westport.
May 15th to 22nd 2019

It took me 10 years to join this wagon and then it took me another 12 months to write this book. So, you should take 12 days to read it.

Acknowledgements

Before I start to compile a long list of the wonderful people who made it possible to prepare this travel book, I would like to mention the major ones, the wonderful Irish people. To write this book was not only inspired by this journey in May 2019 but long before when I lived in Ireland and fell in love with the lot. To acknowledge that fact I think it is best to start with an Irish conversation.

McPaddy was strolling down O'Connell Street when he noticed what he thought was the familiar figure of a friend. Quickening his steps, he came up to the man and slapped him on the back. To his amazement, he then saw he had greeted an utter stranger. I beg your pardon; he said apologetically, I thought you were an old friend of mine, McCarthy by name. The stranger recovered his wind and replied with considerable heat: And supposing I were McCarthy, do you have to hit me that hard?

What do you care, retorted McPaddy, how hard I hit McCarthy?

Special thanks to my old and new friends from Bridport, with whom I spent these wonderful eight days in Westport and without any one of them this book wouldn't have been written. Chinner who never gave up over the last years to encourage me to join the tour and finally he was successful. Ivan St Pierre, I like to thank for his talent and knowledge to organise these tours for so many years. And on tour I had the pleasure to share a great time with J.D. (John Dalton), Steve Johnson, Graham Taylor,

Robbie (Edwin Taylor) (they're not brothers), Grant Connolly, Mark Roe and Colin Poole (That's Chinner☺).

By the way, altogether we counted to 555 years of age (666 would have been a disaster, not only because of superstition, but the 555 kept the average age at 61.7 years and any more here we would have needed some sort of assistance. And many thanks to all the men they went before this trip as the stories mounted up nicely.

Many thanks to all the lovely people over in Ireland. Even the airport staffs stick out with politeness and efficiency for international standards. Many thanks to all the great crew at the Castlecourt Hotel where we lodged this time and of course all the servers and bar tenders in any pub and restaurant we enjoyed. Thank you, Alice from Westport tourist office who gave me the best information, about Westport in just one visit to the office! And special thanks to P.J. for the insider information about the holy mountain.

And I wish to express my deep and lasting appreciation to my friends and associates who have assisted me in preparation of this book. Special thanks to Brian Lovell and Lewis A. Harris from Bridport for the big help to edit the written part of this book. If there might be some mistakes left, it's not their fault but mine. My next book will be in German, I promise ☺. And special thanks to the friends they allowed me to use some of their own photos, Mark and Ivan.

Contents

The people part 1

When nine men plan to do a trip together, they need to form a crew. And here in this case the gang leader is Ivan. Supported and looked after by Chinner. And Robbie does the legal stuff.

Without Ivan I believe all this activity wouldn't have happened. This book would not be available. Ivan is the man behind all of it and he was the first to have the idea to travel together with some friends from the lovely town of Bridport to the wonderful place called Westport in Ireland.

Ivan came to the West Country in Dorset many years ago and lived with his wonderful wife Diana more than twenty years in North Chideock which is only four miles distant from Bridport. They had been married for 55 years when Diana sadly died in 2019.

What I know is that Ivan is a retired Metropolitan police officer. His job then brought him as far as the island of Fiji, where he had to lead an investigation. What impresses me most is that he has sailed on tall ships as a purser too and therefore we always had something in common. His full name is Ivan St Pierre, born in 1940 and he is Irish. That is one reason he travelled so many times over to the emerald island and long before any group went there; Ivan and his late wife were falling in love with Westport already.

Colin Poole from Bridport (55) is one of my best friends since I've live in Bridport and we met first when Chinner, that's how he is known to everybody, joined one of my Jiu-Jitsu classes in 2011 and later the Bridport News wrote "5th Dan for Colin Poole".

Chinner belongs to the "inner circle" of the Westport gang and has been with it already seven times now. Also, he is one of the few who climbed the holy mountain Croagh Patrick. He has been up there twice. Actually, without Chinner this book wouldn't be written, as he cajoled me into it, and I guess after many years of doing it I gave in and joined. What a great choice I made! Chinner is a well-known man in town, born and bred in Bradpole (that's part of Bridport) and I think I can say without hesitation he is the second-best plasterer in Bridport. I don't know who the best one is.

Robbie (69), that's what everybody calls him, but Robert Taylor is his real name. Born in Bridport, lived in London six years, and worked most of his life as local government officer in Dorchester till his retirement at 65. Robbie is our purser, makes sense, he knows all about it. His Westport connection comes through Ivan, and Robbie has now been seven times since his first trip in 2013. He is well travelled all over the world. That includes India years ago, he has been to Canada, Alberta for skiing and to France and Italy also for skiing. Also, he went by train through Spain, stopping here and there.

He enjoys this trip; he finds Westport a friendly place and going there with a crowd of friends is a relaxing break from everyday things. His favorites in Westport are "The Tower" for food, J.J. O'Malleys of course. We didn't go this time.

Robbie likes the Irish music, can sit and listen to that for hours, he says. And the Guinness seems to be better in Ireland than in England, but he doesn't drink Guinness over here, normally prefers bitter.

He says, meeting Matt Molloy that boosted it. Barrack Obama, Bill Clinton, various people well known in the world Matt played for them, it was great to meet him in person at his premises and that inspired the love of Irish music even more.

For those who have no idea where Ireland is and have never heard of the Irish let us start with a joke. During the time living in Ireland, I learned that there are Irish jokes existing among the English in general as there are jokes in Germany about the tribe of the "Ostfriesen" and in Russia about the Chukchee. Okay, I have never met anybody from Chuckotka, but I can tell you that these jokes about the Irish (and maybe about the Ostfriesen) are based on pure jealousy and ignorance. But they are funny…

Paddy is painting his lounge and his wife walks in. "I can't believe how well you're doing Paddy!" Meanwhile the sweat is dripping of him and she says: "Why are you wearing a leather jacket and a coat??" Paddy says: "Oh dear! Read the feckin tin, it says, for best result put two coats on!!"

And it gets worse, as the book goes on… Murphy is with his mate Paddy at the pub. As they got only one € left between them Paddy goes off and buys a sausage. Murphy say are you mad? Now we are skint! Come on says Paddy follow me. And they go into another pub and order two pints and drink them before they pay. Paddy shoves the sausage through the zipper of his jeans and tells Murphy to get down on his knees and suck it.

The barman goes berserk and throws them out. Ten pubs and ten pints later Murphy says: "I can't do this anymore; my knees are too sore, and I am pissed. "How do you think I feel", says paddy. "I can't even remember which pub I lost the sausage in…"

So, be prepared. The faint hearted can close the book and the others can see it's …

Wednesday, 15th of May

Early morning at eight o'clock some of us meet at the Greyhound in Bridport. The Greyhound is a Wetherspoons establishment, that's why they are open this early for breakfast and a pint.

Some friends from town are out and about already and wave us goodbye as we celebrate with a few pints of Guinness to start off things to come.

Ten o'clock was the arrangement to assemble everybody at the "Tiger" in Barrack Street and by 10.30 am we set off in two cars.

Arriving at the airport in Bristol by one o'clock and after everybody passed immigration, we make ourselves comfortable in the departure lounge. This is the first chance to get to know each other for those who are new in the crew.

The departure lounge area at Bristol airport is comfortable and offers a wide variety of good service. Everybody is excited and happy. It is a good start for what is ahead.

Robbie is in charge with the boarding passes; he is our purser and keeps the paperwork up to date. As everybody is a "well traveler" things go smooth and just after two o'clock we're on the plane with priority boarding, wonderfully organized.

Ryan air flight "FRO-202" to Knock, 14.15h, delayed to 14.35h!

Finally, on board the plane we all sit together in three rows, Chinner with Mark and Ivan, Robbie next to Graham and Grant, Horst, Steve and J.D. in the third row. We spoiled ourselves with a few bottles of wine on the plane. The stewardesses had lots to do.

Knock airport

After my personal inbuilt "anti – flying – airport – mode" got already a bit easier with the pleasant experience going through Bristol airport in England, I was wondering how our landing destination in Ireland would be. The rather small jet with his Lithuanian crew circled a few times before the obligatory landing signs came on and we started the final approach. It reminded me instantly of my roughest plane landing so far, which was in the Philippines in 1982 and then I really thought that's it!

But nothing like that. The plane passed in very low altitude what looked like a mixture of farm sheds and small garages which I could reach out by hand, if the windows were open. Rather a feeling of descending in someone's living room than one of these big airport grassland areas. And the plane touched down ever so smoothly and with a big noise the engines brought it to a standstill. Welcome at Knock airport, don't smoke and all this nonsense as known from all flights.

I managed to be one of the first people out and down the gangway and was waiting for our tour leader "Pope" Ivan. As you probably know, when Pope Paul came to visit Ireland about 40 years ago, which was then one of his most important and successful Catholic dependence, he kissed the ground on arrival. And so, did Ivan!

Left in the picture one can see a glimpse of Chinner, who later turned out to be Ivan's right hand. Yes, he really looked after his valuable friend and assisted him wherever needed. Okay, we all helped each other whenever necessary, but this was a special set up.

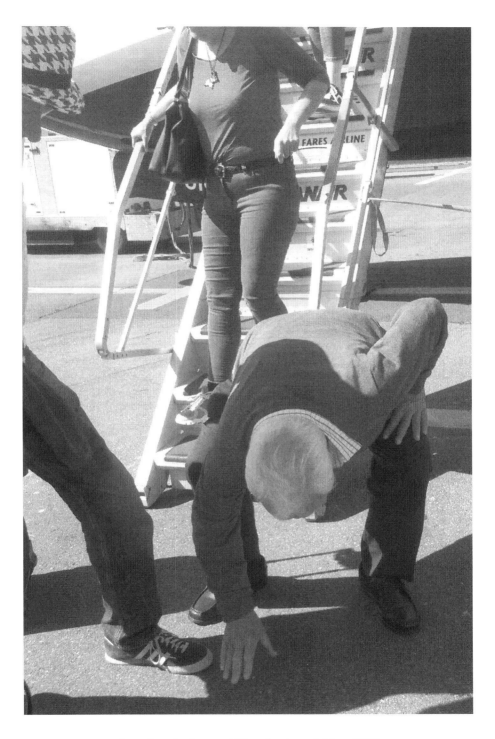

Ivan touch down at Knock airport May 2019

Welcome to Mayo!

Quickly pass the airfield, weather is fine, quick stroll into the main building and show ID to the friendly customs officers. Personal belongings all on board as we all have only some cabin luggage and there is no need to wait for any further baggage to come off the plane.

Everybody is excited and in a great mood. Now we wait for the rented cars to come. Grant and Graham pick them up. I have a little chat with two ladies, they go for holidays too and hope their Irish friends will turn up soon to take them to the lovely place of Sligo, which is a bit further up north from where we're heading to.

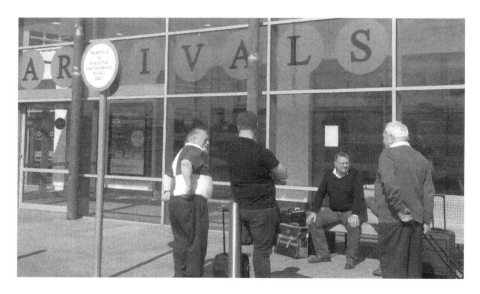

Finally, the cars are here, and we set off. Grant is our driver and the way he does it must be like the Queen's chauffeur; smooth and professional, even on the wrong side of the road, km instead of miles and four over excited passengers on board!

Graham takes care of the second hired car and they have got a bit more space as they are just four of them. Twenty minutes later already we drive into Charlestown. Our first stop is only four kilometres from the airport, and we are heading towards the town centre.

The town seems to be a quiet place this afternoon. A few people are seen doing their business. Not much traffic. We come to the main square and easily enough find a car park. Just over the road it says "J.J. Finan" in capital letters. "Hardware Store and Traditional Pub".

The entrance is in the centre of two big shop windows where it says on the left "Groceries" and on the right "Furniture – Beds – Bedding – Rugs". Above the shop you see an Irish flag in front of a window and on the right, it says, "Central Bar" and underneath the addition "Old World Pub". On the pavement in front we must walk around a wheelbarrow and two metal dust bins. All is for sale, same as the mop and the garden spade.

I think to myself, "Okay, Ivan knows what he does" as he marches ahead, and we all follow in good trust. As we open the door, we recognize that Steve and Grant are already inside and have a good look around. For Bridport readers I just say, you have entered RKL tools! (This is our local downtown hardware store).

Nice store, nice pub, what a wonderful place. Yes, as you walk through this old-fashioned traditional hardware store at the very end is a blue door and behind there opens an even more traditional Irish pub.

I like to state here at this point, that some of the photos I used in this travel book are not to world photographer standards but I believe they give the reader a good idea about the place and if there ever will be a second issue, I promise, I'll travel the same route again and do better pictures.

As we enter the pub there is a warm welcome from a man in his 70s and those who have been here on previous trips with Teds travel know him very well. It is Mr. John Finan, the owner of pub and store which has run as a family business since 1953.

After a very personal welcome we find ourselves some seats while John is preparing already a first round of real Irish Guinness which we've been waiting for so long. Okay, drivers sorry, none. But we will be in our hotel parked up soon.

I must admit, this is a proper pint of Guinness and Mark says it's good to be back on the emerald isle. I wonder if this is the moment where our holiday starts or was that already when we touched the ground at Knock.

Ivan and John Finan have a lot to talk about. Ivan got introduced to this place some years ago by his uncle Seamus Beirne and his brother who was a farmer just outside of Charlestown. This is already the 10th time the group has visited J.J. Finan's pub and as next we get presented the mandatory copy of John Finan's own book "A Little Bit of Ireland". I must tell you that it took me until three months later to start reading it and I find it a very enjoyable collection of real Irish stories, told in a way that you don't want to stop reading them. This time it is Mark, J.D. and me who get a copy as we are visiting here the first time. The book contains thirteen most wonderful and deeply Irish stories, told by a man who can choose just the right words to describe and deliver a deep understanding of the Irish soul and daily life.

If you ever manage to visit this Old World Pub yourself ask John for a copy and he will sign it for you. Others could order one online at www.trafford.com/07-2627, Trafford publishers, by John Finan 2008.

I take advantage and ask John for a short interview and we leave the bar and have a chat over the counter in the warehouse part.

John Finan says: "Short stories, short fiction stories I have written here about people around here, things which happened fifty or sixty years ago. It didn't happen, but it could have happened. I wrote these short stories out of my head.

I watch the people in the bar, and I write down things. And there is a bit of mystery attached. I wrote the book about ten years ago, but the message goes back nearly sixty years."

His pub is famous with the music band Oasis. Guess everybody knows their top songs like "Don't Look Back in Anger" and many more. Oasis's front man Liam Gallagher's late grandmother Margaret Sweeney, who was a popular figure around the pub and the local community of Charlestown lived nearby here.

Gallagher still is a regular visitor to Mayo and every time he comes to visit Charlestown he pops into the local pubs and has played live at J.J. Finan many times.

"Charlestown and its pubs suffer these days a bit with the rural setting and it has made some challenging trading conditions, so regular visits from Gallagher and his friends have helped keep the local bar open. He brought a good few tourists and stag dos in", John Finan has to tell.

John still remembers the emotional impact of Margaret's passing on the local community which is over a decade ago. He tells me that their grandmother Margaret Sweeney was so special to him that the night she died he was crying.

John Finan signs his book "A Little Bit of Ireland"

And John can tell a lot of mysteries and local stories as he is already second generation who runs this dual place, a hardware store combined with a traditional pub.

As we go back in the pub and join the others, John gets his violin out from behind the bar and we can listen to a wonderful Irish fiddle tune from a man who is obviously well experienced with his instrument. After the applause another round of this Irish liquid gold is on its way. Everybody is happy, good atmosphere, lots of Guinness, real Guinness.

Then it's time to set off again as the drivers get itchy, watching us others enjoying the Guinness. We leave in good order and make our way to Westport.

Grant is driving ahead of us and I assume they have the same good mood as in our car. The Irish countryside is flying by and our excitement is even bigger now after that introduction at J.J. Finan world Pub. I sit next to J.D. and he gives us a little idea what he likes to eat. He loves a bit of porridge and sugar. "Porridge is very good for you." And he admits he does like crumpets too. "You get these big ones now, you know? Massive crumpets. They're lovely. They're six inches, how can you get them in a toaster?"

After a good thirty minutes cruise on the motorway N5 we enter Westport.

Pass the first traffic lights and there it is. We turn into the driveway of Castlecourt Hotel just before 7.00 pm. Cars get parked in the underground space and we make our way to check in at the hotel reception.

Booking of the rooms has been already organised by Ivan before we set off and now it's just the ordinary check in, show ID and claim the card key. We booked four double bedrooms and as Ivan is our senior member and tour operator, he can enjoy the comfort of a single room with a big four poster and extra seating area. Now that's a plan where we will have our first Gin party…

Check in at Castlecourt Hotel reception. We are awaited and all goes very quickly and professionally. From the left, Robbie and a glimpse of Grant behind him, Graham, Chinner and Mark.

Luckily, we are all grownups and well-traveled, so it doesn't take long and we all meet half an hour later outside in the spacious courtyard for a happy welcome pint of Guinness!

Then we made our way to the famous pub and music place "Matt Molloy's". And as the digital camera always provides you with the time, I can tell that at 9.15 pm I took the last photo of the day…

Ivan got greeted by Matt Molloy's son Peter who showed us around before the busy night started. What a great place and what a treat for us to look backstage. Very shortly later it was buzzing.

Matt Molloy's it's the 10th time now the groups have visited. But Ivan has been here many times before that.

Mark Roe, Chinner, Matt Molloy's son Peter, Robbie Taylor

They say if you enter a pub blind folded, you still notice that you enter a pub. At Matt Molloy's one needs probably ear plugs as well. You can feel the atmosphere as you walk in. All these many live gigs have left a unique aura in this place.

Now as there are hardly any people at the back rooms one can see all the details. There are photographs of many world-famous people showing up from the walls. Bill Clinton with Matt Molloy, Matt Molloy with Mick Jagger, Horst with, oh sorry, that's missing.

The rooms are decorated with lots of lovely memories from the past. All is kept rather simple and serving the purpose. And soon again hundreds will flood in and enjoy this unique place with the choice of some best Irish music presented.

This is the smoking area at a backstage courtyard. Robbie our chief none smoker does the inspection. When in use the stable door is shut.

This is the main back room where the bigger events happen, and bands entertain the crowds. It has got an extra bar attached to it. And I can tell you – they got busy.

Another dedicated space for musicians only. Must be vacated daily by 9.15

Traditionally we had a round of Guinness to start with and in a very short time the pub was packed, and everybody was looking forward to the music starting. And one honestly can say this place is the best known Westport pub all over the world. It attracts thousands of visitors every year who enjoy the place for the traditional music, dark, deep and unpasteurized like it's pints as they say. Very often Matt Molloy (The Chieftains) is performing too and you can enjoy the heart of the pure Irish music for the price of a pint. Matt Molloy's is with all its fame still quite a small place, authentic and atmosphere rather than gold digging. A must go when in Westport!
http://www.mattmolloy.com/home

Mark and Chinner were last men standing and decided to have a kebab on the way home. BAD IDEA Mark says.

Thursday, the 16th of May

I wake up early and notice the different noises in the morning. Lots of birds, crows instead of the usual Bridport seagulls making their morning concert, and hardly any cars to hear. It's quieter here in the hotel than at my home next to the corner shop in Bridport. I take a selfie at 8am in the bedroom as you do when on holiday and let Robbie have the precedence in the bathroom.

Half an hour later I make my way down to the breakfast reception. I must admit that I was a bit skeptical at this moment, but this is down to my international travels and staying in too many hotels all over the place. And many can be a challenge, never mind how many stars they've got.

"MV Castlecourt" Promenade deck

The alleyways in the hotel remind me of ships corridors, they are very long. Here comes the question to my mind, how I managed to find the right door last night? We are at the 3rd floor and today I decide to take the staircase rather than the lift down to the breakfast area which is located on the ground floor.

On entering the room, I am greeted by a member of staff and she points me to a dedicated place for our group. All nicely prepared, three tables of four means plenty of room for us nine travelers. Nice start of the day.

At the buffet I find my best friend for the next eight days. It is a magnificent toast machine! I have never seen such a thing before in my life and that device does the job. The choice for breakfast is enormous, name it, they have it. And all well presented and looked after. What a relief for me, as I do usually hate hotels with a morning buffet in general.

But this teaches me different. The friendly lady takes the order for a cooked breakfast and shortly after I m spoiled with a large full Irish breakfast. Could have ordered anything really, but I thought as we are in Ireland it's the right choice. And it was!

We sit together and chat about last night's impressions and how much we enjoyed the place. Only one is missing this morning. Mark decided for little lay in. He had one too many as Chinner says. That's fair enough. "Bloody lightweight"! That's what he calls himself later.

Order of the day now is to meet up at ten everybody down in the courtyard. Ivan as our tour guide has planned to introduce us to the beautiful countryside down to the Doolough valley.

Our departure gets a little delayed. J.D. got lost on stairs, which I can understand. The hotel is like a big passenger liner. That's how it feels to me with all the decks and corridors and cabins.

Mark claims to be "ill" as mentioned earlier on and lastly, we have to wait for Chinner, and Ivan says it is the same as last year. Chinner needed to change his trousers when he noticed the sun is out! But we're all in good spirits having got plenty of time anyway and look forward to our exploration.

Grant and Graham are the drivers and they pick up the cars from the underground car park deck and pull up next to us others sitting in the courtyard. Now eight only set off and my first impression driving through the centre of Westport is that of a very nice town. Busy but not hectic and the traffic looks very relaxed. Oh boy, I'm probably a bit disturbed and damaged by living in Bridport too long with its sometimes chaotic and hectic traffic.

From Castlecourt we turned right. Passed the first set of traffic lights and roll over the bridge which connects the towns northern and southern part divided by the Carfrobeg River.

I took this photo through a window. You get an idea of the place.

The whole town looks nice and tidy. They even care for their building sites. At the memorial square we see a site, where they have covered the scaffold with a tarpaulin showing exactly how it will look like after works are done.

What a great way to make a building site look pleasant, everybody is impressed by that. Just opposite where M.J. Hoban used to be, another favorite drinking establishment from previous tours. It's closed now for good. On my next visit four months later, I could take another shot of the square. The similarity is astonishing.

Covered building site with Cobblers bar

The Cobblers Bar after refurbishment

My friends tell me about the Pub "Pat Dunning" as we pass the place where it used to be, and I learn what a wonderful host and lovely man Pat was before he unfortunately died. At his place the group stayed five times on previous trips.

We have a short stop at a flower shop to buy six bunches of different flowers for later when we visit the memorial in the Doolough valley. A few minutes and we leave the town behind us and enter the coast road which is called the "Wild Atlantic Way" and runs all the way along from up north near Malin Head to the south of Ireland where the Atlantic meets the Celtic Sea. In the area around Westport where it covers the county Mayo from Achill down south to Galway it is called the Bay Coast. While the more southern part around Limerick refers to the many cliffs and is therefore named Cliff Coast.

On the right side we can see the beautiful scenery of Clew Bay which is friendly to us this morning and greets us with a proper high tide. The coast road winds along the banks and one can strongly feel the close connection to the Atlantic further out westwards. It is exciting to be close to the open sea especially when living ten years at the rather locked in English Channel at our hometown Bridport.

First view of Croagh Patrick from car

Minutes later we get a first glimpse of the holy mountain. The Croagh Patrick, nearly 3000 feet and an iconic landmark for the Westport area. I was told already all the stories my friends had on previous trips to Westport, when they climbed up there for charity or just for fun. The very first sight of this divine top made me decide I'd have to go up there soon myself.

Chinner tells us that he has been on top of the mountain twice already. Once he was drunk and would not recommend doing so to anyone. The second time they went with a group of four, and the Bridport Palmers brewery among many others sponsored them for charity. But this time he says he will give it a miss; it is not an easy climb up there as he knows.

I knew about his stories already before we came to Westport and had it clearly in mind to go up there. Ivan stopped me doing so and of course I listened to his advice. I can tell you, sometimes it's good to have someone who knows better.

Later in the year we visited Westport again in a small group and only for five days and this time I was prepared to climb the holy mountain Croagh Patrick. My fellow traveler friends Ivan, Rafique Choudhury and B.B. Tim dropped me off at the inn in close visibility of the mountain. As it was a different journey, I don't want to go in details this time because it would fill a book on its own. I only can tell you this, the mountain is holy, it's not a walk up there but a combined climb and crawl and when you're on the top, you can see the 365 islands of Clew Bay. There is one island for each day of the year but not the leap year. And one of the refuges used to be owned by John Lennon.

The author on top of Croagh Patrick with the view towards Clew bay

Croagh Patrick on the left we do a sharp right turn into a little lane which I've been told is the location of the Irish National Famine Monument nearly at the foot of the holy mountain. We pass that for the time being and only two minutes later comes the next memorial. This one is for the fishermen from Mayo who lost their lives at sea. A plain white miniature lighthouse in immaculate condition surrounded by flower arrangements honors those men. RIP brave fishermen!

Fishermen memorial county Mayo

A few more road bends and we arrive at Murrisk Abbey and graveyard. Grant parks up next to a huge stone wall which obviously shall keep the sea out from the abbey grounds. At the metal gate I notice some seaweed which means sometimes they have high tides entering the graveyard. Later I was told by a local visitor at the graveyard that this place can get flooded.

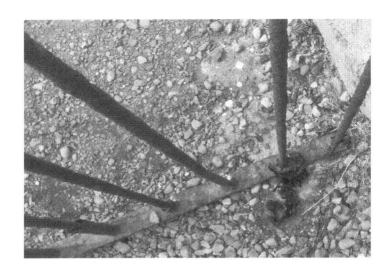

Seaweed at the entrance to Murrisk abbey and graveyard

What a marvelous place to have a graveyard. Sure, if I ever must be buried it should be here. That's a minimum what a navy captain deserves. Right next to the Atlantic!

The remains of the abbey are to the right and I make my way into the cemetery. The ground is about five feet above sea level and spreads out along the bank providing space for more than a hundred graves. I must mention here that visiting graveyards all over the world is one of my passions and this one is probably the hundredth I've been to. And what a unique one!

Cemetery with a sea view

These are the remains of the Murrisk Abbey with Croagh Patrick in the distance hiding its peak in clouds. Our cars parked outside and Grant, Robbie and Steve are exploring the site.

Murrisk Abbey main building without a roof anymore

Near the Murrisk Abbey and cemetery you find a nondescript green bench. Sometimes I believe that this seat carries a little secret which is probably only known by our tour operator "Father Ted". Who is commonly known as Ivan. As soon we parked up, he went straight to this place and took a seat right at the edge of this emerald green painted bench.

He places himself right to the edge and it looks like he is waiting for someone to come and sit with him again here! Ivan has visited this place many times before and looking at him now on his own on this green wooden bench opens many stories from the past.

Croagh Patrick enthroned over the green bench at Murrisk Abbey

It takes some time for the drivers Graham and Grant to collect the whole tour crew. One is still sitting on this bench and me myself I can't get enough of this magnificent graveyard which is the ideal burial ground for a sailor! But there is a lot more to do on our first big drive and finally both cars are heading back towards the "Wild Atlantic Way".

The right hand side enfolds Clew Bay now at its best and it feels like a real engagement with nature by taking in all the beautiful scenery of the "Wild Atlantic Way". The natural vegetation on both sides of the road is resistant to the harsh elements of wind and sea. It is the Atlantic which formed this breathtaking environment. It's a feast for the senses.

Driving through Kilsallagh towards Old Head Beach, we leave the actual coast road and after the little town of Louisburgh a few kilometers further we take a turn to the left heading towards Doolough valley.

Lough Nahaltora, peaceful, quiet, nature pure

The landscape changes as we drive along. Mountains form valleys which host reservoirs of water and wildlife. And while the top of the hills is rocky and bare and without any vegetation the valleys give us an idea why Ireland is called the "Emerald Island". Green is the colour of the day!

Besides a few birds we don't see any other animals than a few cows and it looks like the sheep can run free here as they can't escape anyway.

As we drive along it is a good opportunity to get to know each other a bit better. Steve who sits next to me in the back tells us about the strong gravity at the Castle Hotel. He fell out of bed last night, woke up on floor and was wondering what happened? I tell you what happened, that is down I believe to the hidden influence of the fine Guinness at Matt Molloy's last night! We enjoy each other's company very much and it feels like a good team to travel with. Everybody enjoys himself on this first excursion.

There is hardly any traffic on these lanes but if a car approaches you better stay sharp at the side. Looks like the locals know their way and this appears to be the same as anywhere in the world. The unexpected sheep in the middle of the road put another burden on the drivers' skills.

Then it seems we have lost contact with Graham's car and there is of course no mobile phone signal here to give them a ring. Nevertheless, we manage to arrive nearly same time at our next target which is the famous Famine Memorial at Doolough valley.

The Doolough Famine Memorial, a plain stone cross engraved telling you about the "Doolough Tragedy 1849", as a reminder of one of the blackest events in Irish history.

Many starving people were forced to walk up to twenty miles in harsh weather condition from Louisburgh to Delphi Lodge to attend an inspection and get famine relief. It is supposed that more than 400 people died at Doolough on the journey.

It is engraved: To commemorate the hungry poor who walked here in 1849. Unveiled by Karen Gearon. Dunnes stores strikers. 7.5.94 / erected by AFRI.
In 1991 we walked AFRI's great famine walk at Doolough and soon afterwards we walked the road to freedom in South Africa.

As I believe there aren't any coincidences, I notice the connection of the great famine in 1847 and me living in Drogheda twenty years ago. At a time when Ireland was enduring the terrible loss of a million dead and the mass exodus of a million more during the great hunger, the story goes that the Ottoman Sultan, Khalefa Abdul-Majid, declared his intention to send £ 10,000 to aid Ireland's farmers. However, Queen Victoria intervened and requested that the Sultan send only £ 1,000 because she had sent only £ 2,000 herself.

The Turkish film director Omer Sarikaya produced the movie "Famine" which features this amazing story. The Sultan sent only the £ 1,000 in aid, but he secretly sent five more ships full of food. The English courts attempted to block the ships, but the food arrived in Drogheda harbour and was left there by Ottoman sailors.

This charitable act from a Muslim country to a Christian nation, separated by 4,000 miles, was an unlikely outcome. The Ottoman Empire was experiencing enormous internal difficulty, but the Sultan Abdul-Majid was determined to help the starving people of Ireland. A friendship between two different cultures was formed. The writer and director of "Famine "discussed the film with Mel Gibson who is half Irish, but Gibson's agent denied joining.

I have worked in the new and the old docks of Drogheda and now all these years later I stand in front of the famine memorial which is connected to it.

And it was not only the death toll. In the years between 1846 and 1851 an average of 300 desperate Irish immigrants landed in America every single day!

Ivan with our six bunches of flowers and the memorial at the top left

I can tell this is another important highlight of our tour. Here at the memorial we pay respect to the Irish history which is connected to very much suffering.

The six bouquets we brought back honour the memory of our very own friends and family. Ivan puts the flowers down for his late beloved wife Diane, red roses. I am glad I could meet Diane on many occasions and remember her as being such a nice lady. Graham chose some pink and yellow flowers to remember his late mother-in-law Marion. Mark, who is from Dublin, commemorates his late father Thomas, and Chinner brought a flower bouquet which is for his lovely mother Cath. I am still very fond of her, a lovely lady and mother of twelve she was! Pat Dunning who was not only a host for the travelers for many years and a great pub landlord, but a friend too received similar flowers to those for our late friend Dodge, R.I.P., who has been a team member for so many years.

As we finish our little private ceremony at this memorial a coach arrives to bring a bus load of tourists of which we haven't seen much so far. Time to proceed and now we are heading further south towards the famous Aasleagh Falls.

Here we pass this delightful 1830s country house, which is a fishing lodge and hotel now. This is probably the place if you're after some charming accommodation in glorious scenery with great food and total tranquility. The 1000 acre Delphi estate is one of Ireland's hidden treasures. The historic lodge, famous as a holiday hideaway, is surrounded by the tallest mountains in Connemara and overlooks the lakes and rivers of the Delphi valley famous for their salmon and sea trout fishing.

We take a narrow but good road to drive, obviously repaired recently and with pleasant surroundings. It brings us to the Killary Fjord which we follow eastwards for another three kilometers and arrive at a waterfall which marks the end of the Erriff River before the waters form the Killary Fjord.

There wasn't much rain recently and therefore the waterfall is reduced to a third of its size in comparison to the last visit as Ivan and Chinner confirm. There is an information board which shows the falls in full size and Ivan tells me that's how it usually looks here. "Today it is rather small, actually very small!"

I am still impressed though, watching water masses streaming down and making this unique noise giving you the feeling of an endless energy force. Having visited myself the Niagara Falls in Canada as well as the Victoria Falls in Zimbabwe it comes to my mind that these here are still much bigger than ours in Bridport just outside Netherbury.

Little water this year at Aasleagh Falls

We all swarm out again and each one explores the scenic site in his own way. Chinner tells me a little anecdote, when Dodge read the "P" sign as "piss here" and as he emptied himself behind him there been these two American tourists who pretended they heard the Aasleagh Falls. I think this was about the time somebody asked how long it would take to the pub, as looking at all this water makes you thirsty.

I must confess at this point, that by writing all this sometimes I ask myself if I should consume a few pints of Guinness as I add the lines. Reminds me to one of my several fiancées who was a writer and author of I guess fifteen books then and none was written without the miraculous help of a good red wine. Okay, I leave it here; guess the lector who edits this before printing will delete it anyway.

The scenery of the falls provided the grounds where the ambush scene was filmed for the movie "The Field", directed by Jim Sheridan. The film was shot throughout Connemara and County Mayo around Leenaun and Killary Harbour.

"Where is Robbie?" Robbie explores the site in his own way and doesn't get any of the urge we feel for a pint. "Come on, all in the car, off we go!" He apologises for his delay and tells me that because on previous trips it was only possible to take a photo shot through the open car window due to heavy rain. "We are very lucky today. It's a dry day".

Punctually at 12 noon we arrive at the pub. Ivan told me that the landlord always sits in the window with his back to the road since ever they came there and as we turn into the car park, I can see this massive giant in the window. Ivan was right!

Mr. Padraic Coyne

We are at the Carraig Bar, Westport Road, Leenaun, Connemara in County Galway. Thank god! And drivers! As we enter the bar there is a very hearty welcome. Robbie, Chinner, Grant, Steve and of course Ivan are well known visitors here and again it feels like coming home.

Padraic, that's the landlords name turns out to be not only a very handsome nice chap, but he knows a lot as well about Westport. He tells me some interesting stories about a man called Peter Josh Carty, who is the founder of the Castlecourt Hotel, which is for ten years now run by his son and daughter. Padraic knows about the history of Castlecourt Hotel and tells us lots of details, but unfortunately my Dictaphone wasn't switched on and therefore I have only vague memories of what he really said. That is a shame. I could find out later a few details of the hotel.

The Castlecourt Hotel started in the year 1971 as an eleven bedroom guesthouse by Mai and Petie Joe Corcoran, Padraic knew them from his time in Westport. In 1988 the hotel grew to 87 bedrooms and at this stage the son and daughter Joe and Anne Corcoran took over the running of the hotel. 1999 was a major increase to 164 bedrooms, a leisure centre and a new function room were added.

Today, the Westport Hotel Group now incorporates three hotels, the mother ship, which is the Castlecourt Hotel, the 4 star Westport Plaza Hotel located right next door and the Westport Coast Hotel located at the Quay, Westport's only waterfront hotel.

We buy a pint out of our kitty for the landlady and landlord of Carraig Bar and I truly can say their Guinness is some of the best I've ever tasted. Trying to find out what makes the difference, as this is the question ever since I had the first pint of this black gold, the landlady says:

"You need short pipes and keep them well flushed. Our barrels are right under the bar and therefore the way is short, and the taste is great. And it takes time to pull. Often, they want to speed it up, that ruins it."

We all agree with that and order a second round. Sorry drivers!

Best pint of Guinness at the Carraig Bar in Leenaun

You might think Leenaun is quite far from Westport, but Padraic seems to be well connected and well informed. "Today at five they have live music at Mc Carthy's. You shouldn't miss that!"
And he is right. Irish traditional music is legendary throughout the world. This would be a reason enough to visit the area. We will enjoy our daily dose for sure.

His pub and restaurant are for sale. And if you like to live a little bit remote, on a busy road which brings you some tourists in for business and you have 440.000 Euro cash this pub is for sale. That includes the bar, access to beach, the 3 bedroom cottage, one acre of land and the license comes with it, worth already 70.000 Euro. Padraic's family has run this place for the last 23 years and now they feel time it is time for retirement. Fair enough. Padraic is 79 years old, so I feel again I am a youngster!

What doesn't come with the sale is his fifty (50!) year old Mercedes Benz, which is in pristine condition. Sorry no photo of that, you must go there yourself and take one.

Looking around in the bar you see lots of curiosities at the wall. "Wine improves with age. I improve with wine", it says on one board. And true too, "The smaller the fish, the bigger the lie!" And look, we are in Europe! A cigarette machine! Requires tokens from the bar and one pack is available for 13.10 €.

Some features at the bar and a cigarette machine

The curiosities wouldn't stop inside the inn. At the front you see a pair of wellingtons sticking out from a barrel. The former high visibility trousers are not yellow anymore but all grey and the drum itself appears to be from last century. All rusty and worn out. I imagine this was a fisherman who didn't make his way home after the pints.

This probably happens after a seven course Irish meal; six pints and a potato. You go headfirst and imagine the topless mermaid is coming to you.

What it probably is, the left scene is overlooked by a young mermaid with scales and bare breasts leaning on what I guess is a lighthouse. The fisherman should have taken his bearings from her.

Further right there is something which looks like a doll house. A solid thatched cottage only ten feet high and you wonder who resides in there?

The views are stunning! One looks down to the lough with the majestic mountains in the far distance.

So, if you feel you should buy an original Irish inn, here it is. Only 440.000 € to pay for.

On the way back we stop at another memorial, this time because Ivan needs a wee, clever bastard. He just said, "stop here!" But then mind you, not uninteresting at all. I read a Gaelic engraving only on the front, 1921 that's all I understand but luckily at the side it says in English "erected to the memory of the West Mayo Brigade IRA who fought here against British forces 2.6.21". Of course, Ivan knew that!

Afternoon at nearly three o'clock we turn back to the Castlecourt Hotel. I am in a car with Chinner and Grant as driver, Ivan sits in front with him. Another smooth drive. Thanks Grant!

Back at the base everybody takes some time off before some of us meet up outside in the courtyard. Chinner has done his back yesterday and therefore made an appointment for a massage this afternoon with the hotel's private physiotherapist. Ivan buys us a round of drinks to say thank you to the drivers of the day and the good company.

J.D. is planning to play some golf later in the day and now he sits inside the bar with Graham and Steve doing the bar riddle. It reads on a wooden board "ASDTWLCITCOSY" *. Ok, beyond my abilities, but the boys can crack it. This must be a skill in their genes since the U-boat code crackers with the cryptanalysts of the Enigma ciphering system, which enabled the western allies in WWII to read the Morse coded radio communications of the Axis powers that had been enciphered using Enigma machines.

* Meaning: "A Small Donation To Westport Lions Club Is The Cost Of Satisfying Your Curiosity."

Talks are around rugby, which can be watched on a big screen inside the bar and as Mark says "I like rugby" I can see they all do. Not least of whom our friend Graham, who is the landlord of the Bridport pub "Tiger" and that's where most of us meet regularly and enjoy rugby too on one of the big screens.

Chinner returns from physio and he is a happy man now. He is very pleased with the service. 55 € but worth it he says.

Still early day and it is a lovely afternoon in May, and we are in Westport! Finish the one pint sitting in the sun, Ivan, Grant and I decide to have a stroll downtown. As we leave the hotel reception, a group of school kids' queue on the other side of the road. I notice that they wear similar uniforms to those of English schools here.

By walking the streets now in daylight, I can tell how clean and tidy this place is. The pavements here are spotless and I remember that I noticed the same when I first came to my new hometown Bridport from the city of Berlin, some thirty years ago. Today Bridport is rather a mess regarding their pavements. One big difference is probably the fact, that Bridport has got a massive number of dogs nowadays, while Westport seem to be rather dog free. I leave that mosaic here for the reader to appreciate a clean foot path in any town.

At the south end of Castlebar Street where the Castlecourt Hotel is located, we enter the bridge over the Carrowbeg River and just opposite is our first port of call, "The West".

A pub serving the public since 1901

Grant on the bridge linking James Street and Newport Street named "The Doris Brothers Bridge"

As a former hackney driver, I notice the special parking bay for the Westport horse and carriage taxi service. Very pleasant that is.

And as we wait for our first Guinness to settle in the glass Robbie and Ivan walk through the door and join us.

I took that photo through the window as you can see the pavement in the mirroring glass. Couldn't resist going out over the road and trying one of their ice-creams. Choc mint, always my favorite and over the many years enjoying this kind of ice cream I can assure you, this is the very best I ever had. No, not at all because of the possible taste irritation mixed with the Guinness, but this one is highly recommended. If they were on trip adviser with that corner shop, I would give clearly five stars for selling the best very creamy choc mint ice cream with chocolate chunks as big as coins in it.

On the corner I notice two men standing together and offering some brochures to the passersby. Can't believe it as they wear yellow visibility vests and I assume they are Jehovah witnesses. To clarify that, I go and ask and learn that they ask for donations towards the "Women cervical check scandal". The vests have to be worn here by law in this case.

On return I notice that Grant made himself very comfortable in the window seat and Ivan is extremely happy as he went out at the same time and got this trip lottery tickets. Always the same amount according to the number of men in the group. This time we have fabulous 94 € worth tickets. Wait for later!

Grant enjoys time at "The West"

Ivan presents the 2019 trips lottery tickets. Worth 94 € to begin with

At this time of the day the pub is already heaving with people who enjoy the great atmosphere. Most are locals as I notice. Jean and Mary who just finished the day's work in one of the offices opposite tell us they are here every time after work to socialise and meet up with friends. I ask myself, is this now a sort of a time travel experience? That's what it used to be thirty years ago in Bridport when at five o'clock the brick layer stood next to the lawyer and had a conversation with the bar tender at the George Hotel in town. Refreshing to see this kind of real community live still exists over here. In Bridport today much of community life means dancing around a newly planted tree or collecting some donations for charity. Here in "The West" they seem to be aware what over intensive tourism can do to a place and one local named Billy Allan, you will read more of him later, makes it very clear that they can live without us British visitors. Hahaha, he didn't realize I was a German, Ivan Irish and Grant from New Zealand.

One has to understand all the manias of unresolved nationalism, of sexual repression and of hyper Catholicism made the Irish different, distinctive and, in their own estimation at least, charmingly colourful. When you understand this background, you have to love them even more.

We decide it is a good time now to proceed towards Matt Molloy's just for a change and I have the feeling this is part of the ritual on the trips to attend the flagship of Westport music pubs. On arrival we bump into our friends Graham and Mark. Now I know who Ivan has been on the phone with earlier on. He is our tour leader and mastermind to keep the level of quality entertainment and enjoyment up as it was on each tour.

That night I learned that our friend Graham Taylor was such a good entertainer. He introduced us to a few pub games, little jokes (A man, shocked by how his buddy is dressed, asks him, how long have you been wearing that bra? The friend replies, ever since my wife found it in the glove compartment). They would cheer you up with no doubts. I liked best the one with the four coins, but that gets too detailed here now. I only know that four € ended up in my pint glass…

Graham explains the right handling of € coins

Another good one is the Gin test versus Guinness. Mention the Gin; yes, we changed by now to Gin & Tonic with lots of ice and lemon.

And as the drinks get bigger so do the ideas. Mark and I have a mind to climb up this holy mountain, which both of us have seen yesterday for the first time as we drove by on the way to the valleys. Ivan insists if he would go up there, he would die, and Graham wants us to take some flowers for the ancients.

Forgive me here as I cannot tell which band was on that night as we went on with Gin and Tonic later. Around eight o'clock it looks like we had reached some limit today and as Ivan orders a taxi, Chinner, Mark and I join him and roll back towards the castle. While Ivan heads towards his four-poster bedroom, Mark, I, and J.D. who we catch up with at the reception decide on a meal at an Indian restaurant. Out we go again! I was told that Graham had left Mat Molloy's too and was seen at next door's drinking establishment. As he runs his own popular pub and guesthouse "The Tiger" in Bridport, he has a specialised interest looking at the pub scene in Westport to find out how they do it over here.

I notice at this point, that my previous concerns that such a group travel would be too cliquey were totally unjustified. The opposite is the case, and everybody behaves grown up and does what a man does. His own business!

Our choice for the Indian is just around the corner from the hotel the "Olde Bridge Restaurant" at 37 Bridge Street. We manage to have a table on the first floor and although it is already dark outside, it feels nice to sit next to the window.

We three love Indian food and this place is just the right choice tonight. Very tasty food. We got various Indian dishes and one Thai to share, all delicious, and poppadum of course as a starter with some lovely dips. After a day on Guinness and G&T, pebble dashed as Chinner calls it; we now choose some Italian red wine to go with the meal which is of superb quality and very reasonable price too. Just finished the starters there comes Chinner and joins us... great day that was.

On return to my base at room 303 I find out that my mate Robbie who I share the accommodation with is still out and about. Next day I learn he stayed towards the end at Matt Molloy's as the live music was awesome.

The people part 2

Horst, 65 years and German born with an English penchant since early childhood. I live at present in Bridport and before that I lived and worked in six other countries each over a year including Germany. I have a liking for the Irish since I spent twelve months in the country, supervising the distribution of gas pipelines from Drogheda to Galway in the West and down South to Limerick. That was the time I learned "dia dhuit", "go raibh maith agat" and of course "slainte!" OK, "slan go foil".

I am not married, because the Irish women knew I would leave the country after finishing the gas pipe job. And they like to marry someone who stays…By the way, this book is not meant to be serious, it is more a nice diary for us nine who set out to the emerald island in May 2019 which was a fine month for travelling.

J.D. / That stands for John Dalton
(Instead of using my own words to describe J.D., I give you the interview to read instead)

JD: What sandwich have you got?
Me: Ham and salad.
We drink a pint. Cheers, all the best! He says.
Me: You played in a band?
That was in 1978.
Me: You 78 years old?
JD laughs. No! I will be 60 next year in January.
Me: That's a youngster.
He: So they reckon
Me: Yes in our group here, the average is 67!
JD: So Mark is the youngest.
Me: Yes, he messes it up.

How old is he, 45?

Me: no no, 35.

Me: Which band was it, what kind of music?

JD: We didn't do own music; we've done all covers. Simon and Garfunkel stuff, all that kind.

Me: Did you play an instrument?

JD: No no, I was just the singer.

Me: Is there anything still existing of the band?

No, it was a four piece band, four people in a band (bright Scottish accent he has!). One of them died already fifteen years ago, the others are not into music at all anymore.

Was that all in … Scotland?

Yes.

Me: Did you have any groupies?

Yes! The girlfriends at the time, I suppose. I must admit, I really enjoyed it.

Me: Where are you living?

In Bridport, we are only two years now in Bridport. Before that we lived for eight years outside Bridport. In Broadwindsor, that's near Beaminster. But in between we lived in a small village outside Blandford me and wife.

Why Bridport?

That was mainly because of our kids. Two are in Cornwall one lives over in Poole, so we went in the middle. My wife is a dementia nurse over in Weymouth where her office is.

Then Mark (35) turns up and says he got the sandwiches for me, ready at the bar. I go and get them; I say to J.D. Mark will continue the interview. No no! Okay then, switch it off. Where? At the red button. He: I haven't got my glasses on. Okay, I do that.

Graham Taylor
19.05.19 / Room party, 6 o'clock club
"Turn the music down."

Me: "We are having a room party now. I have to catch up now with the interviews and I can't catch Graham later when he is busy with his pub and so on."

Chinner: "We have only started last year, the room party, and 6 o'clock club when Graham bought the Gin. Needs a bit of preparation. This year we get it in their room, not mine."

Everybody laughs

Graham: "For Germany! Preparation prevents piss of a performance."

Me: "Graham, did you mention it? We got nearly £ 19. Do you want to make it to 20?"

Chinner: "Don't mention it."

Everybody is laughing and cheering, all obviously nicely tipsy. Graham sings a loooong "why are we waiting" as in the war which is forbidden to mention".

Then I learned a new word. Connotation.

Graham: "You been on that boat? Das Boot! I have to say, when we are coming away, no one is here to judge anyone, just have a good time."

Chinner: "Never judge a book by its cover."

Me: "But, being German (all laugh). Somebody had the idea; take a German and he will do it."

Graham: "I have to say, I'm absolutely gobsmacked Horst, we all here to have a laugh."

Chinner: "Thank you so much Mr. Taylor!"

Chinner: "Ivan is on his way, if he can make it, upstairs. And we are having a chat, he will love this."

Graham: "As long he's not farting."

Chinner: "I sat next to him and he was farting and Rafique thought it was me".

Graham interrupts the shit talk and offers all: "Cheese and biscuits anybody?"

Chinner: "You don't want to hear this eh? Because I got a bit of wind. But Paddy had a bit of wind, and it sounded like (he makes the noise) and he shit across the bed."

(Graham still tries to stop that conversation.)

It gets hard to have an interview or taping now as everybody talks, slightly under the influence, very interesting to listen at the vibration actually and a very good mood in the room. I try to be serious and continue interviewing with the Dictaphone.

"Come on have biscuits."

Chinner talks about Paddy, ex SAS, (but that's wrong, too many Paddies) he meant a different one. Dodge's friend with the plumber......, lived opposite me. Difficult to hear what they say as everybody stuffed biscuits in the mouth.

Me: "Graham interview ..."
(Ridicules that I still believe this is going to work, this is my 4th time)

Me: "What made you go?"

Graham laughs. "You mean why I joined; I like that. Your English is very good. I was asked by this gentleman here."

Me: "So, you heard about it in the pub?"

Graham: "They said would you join us to Ireland, yes I would actually."

What's your age? My age? I am 67. 67? Surprised me. And you are married to Jackie obviously. When did you come to Bridport?

Graham:" Twelve and half years ago."

Graham switched now to be effective and official, which obviously helps my useless attempt to get an interview under these circumstances.

"We came from Crawley in Surrey. We had a pub there, called the Gatwick. Gives a bit of a clue, because it was next to Gatwick airport."

Me: "Makes sense. Would be funny if you called it Heathrow, next to Gatwick.

Everybody laughs. "Horst has got humour!" Graham likes that.
But then he understands I mentioned is that near Heathrow. Everybody has a laugh, we are pissed. Chinner went there years ago. Gatwick Arms and never realized it was Graham's before they came to Bridport."

"What did you bring to Bridport? Jackie, I brought Jackie and Emily."

"I think that got lost in translation" (guess Graham knew that already, but that's our fun)

Now I say: "What made it go to you to come to Bridport?"

Graham:" Jackie and I were looking to buy a free house".

Me: "We just were lucky to have you. You looked up online and found a pub in Devon, but then it was Bridport. And a free house is better than a Palmers pub."

Graham: "We looked at a place called Oldesham Arms; the place called Oldesham (Devon). But the Devon place was a bit of a shithole and as we were down here, we had a look around at others and one of them was the Tiger Inn."

Chinner stretches his legs out on the bed. Graham says: "Stretch that out! Then we looked at a couple of more and one of them was the Tiger Inn."

"Did you say Tiger tank as in …?"

Graham: "No, not the war machine."

Me: "Hahaha, got you £1!"

Then Chinner asks: "Did he just mention the war?

Hahaha, another £!

Me: "Graham, you have mentioned the word now nine times, do you realize?

Him: "Hahaha, at least we won! And we didn't start it; it was 39 when you invaded Poland."

Me: "Ok, that's enough now. Or is there something else as we hear, let your heart flow."

Me: "You obviously like it, as you here already five times."

Graham: "Yes its fine men. And it's a shame we haven't got Rafique with us. That's about the Queen he went."

(Here I must add that our friend Rafique is next to Ivan and Chinner one of the most frequent travellers to Westport. This time he unfortunately could not take part, as him and his wonderful wife Helen were invited by the Queen for the annual garden fete 2019. There is a lovely picture showing them both there, will hope I can add it here for the reader.)

Friday, 17th of May

Friday morning looks a bit grey from what I can see from my bed. Robbie got up before me and is still in the bath, so I take my time and have a little snooze.

The breakfast prepares us for another day with excitement. Veronica our dedicated waitress in the mornings looks ever so well after us. She turns the breakfast experience into that pleasant status where you feel home and yet get served on a holiday. Veronica asks us where we're going today. Fishing, to Keem bay today? J.D. says: "Not today, we are going to the island." Oh, just to the island, sharks are what you have to look for today. Hopefully you will see them, they are seven meters long. J.D.: "Blimey, that's a long length, seven meters long. Veronica laughing: "Blimey too, on a day like this."
Veronica turns out to look after us very well and professionally and I am more than happy to mention it here and have made an entry on trip adviser too.

All the boys sound a bit rusty this morning from the drinks the night before.

10.30 am. We are already assembled in the underground parking as it is still slightly raining. Today I join in Graham's car, together with Robbie who sits in the front and Steve and me at the rear.

We leave Westport town after a short bit of car sightseeing and turn on the N59 towards north.

As both cars look the same, it's the driver which makes them different. But not only this, Grant's one has got the 007 number plates. Of course I thought, doesn't he look like the perfect London Mafiosi? Maybe that explains why a Garda Síochána, which is the version of an Irish policeman later the day, asked who that man is…?

Graham's car might have a number plate too, but to keep it simple everyone just calls it the DCB. That means "Deaf C… Bus". The name was given as we drove along, and Steve asked a question at Graham who replied that he is driving and can't reply to that in the minute and Steve doesn't hear him at the rear and says "what"? To which Robbie answers "I didn't hear what he said either". The only logical reply from Graham had to be "this car is a DCB". Whereupon I asked what that might mean.

Most of the countryside is divided into private slots alongside the hills. And there are plenty of pink Rhododendrons at this time of the year. I have never seen this many and learn, that they are actually not only a crop plant but grow wild here and cover miles of the usually empty landscape. Originally it is an Asian plant which made itself home in Ireland.

Clew Bay on the left with its many islands we pass Mulranny which was Ireland's best destination for responsible tourism award 2016 and Ireland's best small tourism town, a hidden treasure of spectacular landscapes.

Keeping on the main road we drive towards north and reach the bridge over the Achill sound which connects the mainland with Achill Island.

This is the largest island off the Irish coast and some 60 square miles in size. It is very suitable for hill walking and its beaches and several lakes are a haven for water sports enthusiasts.

I notice plenty of empty properties. Windows and doors are out and often even the roof is gone. There must have been a time when this area was more populated. Today the population is mainly concentrated on the few villages we pass through. But the place still offers a wide range of restaurants and quality accommodation.

Plenty of abandoned houses stand like grey dots in the open countryside.

We pass the small town called Keel which has got an excellent golf course overlooking the Atlantic and we come back to later for the Amethyst bar.

There is still a lot of peat cutting around the island. But it hasn't got the same importance any more than in history, when every farmer had his own turf bank. Then a week's back breaking work in spring provided the family with enough fuel for a year! They say that champion turf cutters could work so quickly that they kept six sods in the air at once. I would love to see that! Nevertheless the turf cutting is next to sheep farming a major income on Achill Island which you can reach by car, as there is a bridge over the Achill Sound.

The "Wild Atlantic Way" tourism board provides the visitors with useful information about this trade all along the way.

The road is very scenic, and we stop to enjoy the view and nature so close to the ocean. Lucky visitors we are today as only a light breeze is out there and a fairly sunny day.

We stop for a group picture and lovely memory. From left Robbie, Mark, Horst, Chinner and Grant. And yes, it was warm enough for shorts!

The sheep are everywhere. And as they say, the grass is always greener on the other side of the fence. Here it seems to be greener the steeper the cliff. But they can manage well it appears.

We all take lots of photos and I have a brilliant video which should go to the end of the book as a CD. Everybody enjoys it to be out and about and Chinner does a step dance on the grass land (see CD).

Few kilometers further we get the first sight of today's final destination. To the left of the winding coast road lays the magnificent Keem bay.

Yes, we can do coffee! Ivan and Grant on the left, Steve hands in pocket, Mark hands on face and Graham hand on imaginary pint of Guinness

Keem bay has a marvelous sandy beach. Very tranquil here. There is only one wooden bench set up and the council only allows one single mobile van down here which sells coffee, soft drinks, light snacks and a common choice of what tourists might like. I ask the salesperson about Guinness and he shakes his head "Oh no, the council wouldn't allow that!"

He tells me that out of season, as it is mid-May, there aren't many visitors here. Mind you, I quite like that because in the summertime he reports the beach is heaving with guests. The bay is very popular among the locals and of course there are more tourists from further away in the summer season. What I find amusing and that is in my eyes pretty much an Irish move, the public toilets are about 300 meters up the cliff.

There is a connection to Achill Island which I find interesting from the German point of view. At the northern end of the island near Dugort beach is a place of interest. It's a cottage called "The writer's residence". In recent years, a huge number of writers and artists have made the journey to Achill Island to stay in the "Heinrich Boll Cottage", which the German writer (Heinrich Böll, 1917 –1985, one of Germany's foremost post WW II writers) bought in 1958 and lived there periodically.

http://heinrichboellcottage.com/

He was a great lover of the Irish and the Irish way of life and the Irish countryside inspired him to take refuge in Achill. His attachment to Ireland was deep and his "Irisches Tagebuch" (Irish Journal), published in 1957 got translated into English 10 years later.

All this propelled German visitor to this country, particularly to Achill. Ireland is very popular among German liberals. I remember when my youngest son visited me during my stay in Drogheda in 2003, just by mentioning his intention to spend a holiday in Ireland, his schoolteacher set his school notes right up two scores.

And Böll being asked, if he believes all the Irish are half crazy, he replied diplomatically: "No, I only think half all Irishmen are half crazy. Two of his novels may be well known to the reader, "The Clown" and "The Lost Honour of Katharina Blum", which we had to read at school, and I remember I hated it then. But with his Irish connection which I only found out while researching Achill, I made my peace with it.

As we sit all relaxed and happy at the viewpoint's only benches Ivan reminds us of the kitty. We will soon need it filled up properly when we attend the Amethyst Bar at Keel on the way back and it doesn't look alright if we walk in there and collect the money then.

During the drive back we enjoy again the stunning views and nature at its best with the ocean on one side and the unspoiled Achill wilderness. I learn from Ivan that our next destination, the Amethyst Bar in Keel is one of the regular spots since the group travels began. Only in 2016 it was closed as the whole building was demolished for refurbishment.

We park up on the main road and enter the pub through an archway door and experience another friendly and warm welcome. Although this time it seems there are different staff to previous year's visits. But that kind friendliness followed us anywhere we went so far. I know that from my year living in Ireland that this is the very Irish own tradition and way of life.

Seven pints of Guinness, one coffee and one shandy is the first order. By the way, a pint of Guinness costs 4.30 €. You wonder why most places in Bridport charge ruthless £5 for a glass, which is in comparison only dearer but nowhere close to better.

A photograph inside the pub reminds of the demolition day in September 2016

I asked Ivan if there ever been any women with them on tour.
His short answer was: No female on tour.

Finish our second round (we never have just one!) time to move on and drive back to the castle even more relaxed now than on the outbound tour. In the hotel everybody takes some care of themselves and we have already arranged that we want to join Matt Molloy's tonight for some life music.

Meanwhile there is a wedding reception held at the courtyard of our hotel but still plenty of space for the hotel guests. All is beautifully arranged with flower bouquets and lots of food on long tables for the party. By looking at the many elegant dressed and attractive people one of us can't help himself but to say: I wish I would be younger!

Graham watches the live rugby on the big screen inside the "Petie Joe's Bar", which is the name of the hotel bar, so do Steve and J.D. who have an endless talk about their beloved hobby while enjoying a drink at the bar.

To give you an idea of the prices I mention a few orders we had there. Pint of Guinness: 4.30 €, 3 Tonic water: 6.60 €, 1 Soda water: 2.20 €, 7 Cork dry gin: 32.20 €, 1 pint Orchard Thieves: 4.70 €, 7 pints of Guinness: 30.10 €. It is all reasonable and affordable when on holiday.

Half past six is departure time for Matt Molloy's from the hotel. Has to be fairly early to arrive there and reserve best seats at the back as Ivan knows. On arrival we enjoy a few G&T's at the front bar but for later we have arranged the places for the music at the rear to make the most of it. Tonight it is "Crookedtrad" which is at the time the most popular house band at the premises.

The room for tonight's gig is at the very far end of the large pub and has got a small stage and there is a separate bar to the left of it. We managed to sit very close to the musicians in the right hand corner. The hall is filling up quickly with a big crowd of happy and cheerful spectators and the bar staff whiz through the rows to collect already the first empty pint glasses. We too switched to Guinness in the meantime and it proves that we are in the right place to have an uninterrupted flow of this magnificent liquid.

Just before eight o'clock the room is packed with approximately 120 people and the professionals on stage begin their tune. Wow! What an amazing atmosphere there is now.

Later during the evening Mark's family arrives and joins us at the table. Makes me laugh as Robbie offers his seat to Mark's sister, but her young boy takes it. Oh well, modern times☺. The band has their very own CD for sale at the front of the stage and Chinner buys one. The mood is exuberant, and a few people begin to dance and Chinner joins them with some talent.

Ivan gets called out in memory of our late friend Dodge and starts crying. But then he says to us: "All good boys"! Meanwhile Chinner tries to convince the band leader to swap T-shirts. His Crookedtrad T-shirt changed for Chinner's white English O2 shirt. No chance! Damn! The kitty is finished and from now on each to their own! Chinner gets a round G&T's and one Tullamore D.E.W. whiskey.

Then he blames me for having a bad breath as we have to talk quite closely because of the noise from the live music. But we pretty quickly learn that Ivan had let out a fart. Pete, or better Peter who is Matt Molloy's son joins us in the corner and we really feel right at home by now.

And now it comes! The next song is called "I don't like Mondays". Hardly anybody keeps sitting and Chinner joins the few dancers at the front again as this is his personal number one favorite tune.

After this one we get a taste of the probably best pipe performance one can get of the Irish music. The guy is supposed to be one of the most famous Irish pipe players. I think his name was Jess Cavity. Forgive me if I got that wrong, but I am more somebody who enjoys the music and hardly ever knows who is performing.

Sometime around midnight I find myself back in the hotel. Robbie seems to be still out and about. That was day three, another good one on this trip!

Saturday, 18th of May

Early rising for me this morning and I notice again the murder of crows outside performing their morning ritual squawking. I quite like it as it makes a change from hearing the boring seagulls in Bridders all over again.

My roommate Robbie seems to be back as I can tell from the snoring noises coming from the next bed. Luckily snoring doesn't bother me as I can blank the tone out with my white magic skills. Others are less fortunate. J.D. shares with Steve who proves to be the master snorer and J.D. finds it hard to get rest, so he decides to spend half a daytime in bed to catch up with some beauty sleep. Graham and Grant share one suite and nothing to report from there, they're obviously less troubled by this problem. Other than Chinner and Irish Mark, who says never again will he share with Chinner as he wakes him up at night with the snoring Olympics. Ivan is the happy bunny (or one of us?) as he just shares his room with four posts. As tour operator he has a single room with a four poster and the daily complementary bottle of red.

So far we had lots of sunshine and it looks like there might be a bit of rain out there today. We will see, first another of the soul and body feeding breakfasts at the Castle Court.

I am somewhat fascinated with the hotel's toast machine. Yes, it is a machine rather than an ordinary toaster. You can put up to four slices on a conveyor belt like grill, it runs through the inside where is I guess a hell like heat and drops the perfect toasts out at the bottom. Now I can understand why this guy at the next table had ten pieces of toast yesterday.

For the last few days we had our personal waitress at breakfast. Today Veronica deserves some time off and we miss her friendly professional service, the way she looks after the whole group every morning. As a result the tables are not arranged in the same way and therefore each of us sits alone somewhere all over the restaurant. I end up in the right hand corner, the only one which was comfortable for me and vacant. From here I have a good view to contemplate other guests having their breakfast. You can learn a lot by watching people and how they behave at the table.

There is this lady left of me who pretends to be posh. But only she looks stiff and tight sitting over some pale scrambled egg and tea without milk. A young man near the window shovels the fruit in like a mill; while his girl opposite him is texting the world probably about what she is having for buffet. And it must be the influence of this toast machine. Two men got themselves each at least ten slices on the plate and one actually manages to eat them all. No one to be seen of our gang so far. I must be in early. But then I remember Ivan saying Saturday is a "day off". Guess they have a lay in.

Later returning from my room I attend in the courtyard and Robbie sits with J.D. out there in the morning sun having a little chat.

J.D. and I decide to have a stroll through town. See where it goes, we don't have a clear direction to start with. Maybe have a look at the Westport House or even make it down towards the harbour?

Leaving the hotel through the drive and heading to the town centre. We pass McCarthy's, I think that's the place the group used to stay many times before. J.D. and I wouldn't know as we are novices on this trip. Walking past the Octagon square with the monument we make the choice to continue through the park in front of us which leads to the famous Westport House, which is one of the Westport's attractions. We didn't go in this time, but J.D. returned another day to do so. The place was built in 1730 on top of another big house which was there since the 15th century. Today it is home to the Hughes family, and they open it to the public. Thirty rooms to see with thousands of pieces of original artwork, artifacts and architecture. It's located in a beautiful landscaped park with huge old trees and healthy looking green grass. A flock of fifteen sheep made themselves comfortable under a huge tree as it had started to rain lightly.

J.D. and I ignore the weather and want to make a visit to the harbour. J.D. has his reasons. I simply always go and see the harbours. Old habit from my time on the boats, I guess.

Right hand of the path we stroll along is the Westport House Lough which is the very end of the Carrowbeg River running through the town centre. I assume it is connected to the sea further up north behind some woods but must be regulated by a kind of lock as inside the lake water is at full height and opposite towards the sea, we can see its low tide this morning.

Where the park changes into the harbour area we recognize the old lifeboat station. Previously it was housed in a wooden chalet, which is not in use anymore and looks a bit run down. It seems to be from hundred years ago. Nice piece of maritime history for me to look at.

Only a few boats at the inner site of the pier and our views go to the long buildings to the left. These are all former warehouses from the time when Westport used to be a very busy fishing port. Today they are all neatly done up and, from what I can see, with shops and restaurants on ground floor and apartments in the top three or four floors.

There is plenty of parking at the front and I'm curious and check about the tariffs. Three € per day and 60 cent an hour it says. We notice the Helm, a pub and restaurant and at the very end is a big blue painted building housing the Towers which is one of Westport's recommended seafood eateries. I am glad we did visit both of them later during the tour for some exceptional dining.

As we're not quite sure how long and which way it will take us walking back, we turn around and head towards Westport again. The main road between Westport harbour and town centre reminds us very much at our Westbay Road in Bridport which connects harbour and town there. The weather has changed again to blue skies and the sun is out and we enjoy the views between the houses in the surrounding countryside.

Pass by at an estate agents window and one of the offers says 299.000 € for a 4 bedroom and 3-bathroom family home, high quality new built and walking distance to town. Bridport readers can compare what that means to our prices… Back downtown and passing the bridge which connects north and south side I notice a plate saying, "Doris Brothers Bridge". This crossing bridge is named in honour of William and Patrick J. Doris.

The Doris brothers made significant contributions to the social and political development of County Mayo in the late 19th and early 20th centuries. William Doris helped draft the famous "No Rent Manifesto", which is one of the major documents in Irish history and he and his brother co-founded the Mayo News, which is Westport's newspaper today. Through the Mayo News they fought the injustices of the landlord system and British rule in Ireland.

Arriving outside the hotel we bump into Chinner who is on his way to town. Quick decision, I join him. We pass the tourist office and I learn now it is called "Discover Ireland Centre". Quick look at a parking meter in town: same tariff as the one at the harbour. Chinner shows me a bike hire shop I might be interested in as one of the owners is a German. It's called Paddy and Nelly and a minute later we are in the pub next door, called Mc Carthy's.

Looks like Chinner came home. Everybody greets us and Chinner introduces me to some of his friends from previous trips. While Chinner is having a dance, I get challenged by another Paddy for some wrestling style Irish folk dance. Then I witness a kind of a pub record. Chinner makes a bet with one folk to drink up the pint within two (2!) seconds. Gulps and gone. That's new even for me as a weathered sailor. Two seconds, this is obviously a record for the Guinness (book of records).

I got challenged for a little bit of pub wrestling

Such a fun afternoon and you can tell this is only the beginning.

Chinner has a bit of a moment and then he likes us to move on next door for a game of pool. Ok, I' m not that kind of keen pool player but always interested in exploring different places. Not far from Mc Carthy's we walk into what's called Cosy Joe's Bar. Bright red painted from the outside and secretly darkish as we enter. We make our way to the back room and lay siege to the pool table.

"I told you I'm crap at it!" But Chinner takes it with a smile as he beats me the second time, leaving all of my balls on the green.

Just as my friend sets it up for my possible revenge, another guest enters the table and shouts out loud "Chinner! I knew it was you. I heard you laughing from next door at the bar!" You won't believe what kind of overjoyed and jubilant merge that was. Two old mates seeing each other again. This is called more than unexpected. Must be pre-vision!

Chinner reaches out to his friend and they both rest for a long while in a big manly hug. After that the guy musters me and shouts out, he can't believe! "Are you Barry McGuigan"? For a short moment I start to believe it myself again. During my year living in Ireland and travelling the most parts of it I was identified countless times as my famous Irish super star boxer Barry McGuigan *. Check it out yourself, can't use a photo here because of copyright and all that.

https://www.google.com/search?q=Barry+McGuigan&rlz=1C1C HBD_en-GBGB800GB800&source=lnms&tbm=isch&sa=X&ved=2ahUKE wis2fCSnpDpAhUOTRUIHd3oDw8Q_AUoAXoECBYQAw&bi w=1920&bih=937

We are just looking like identical twins. "No, no"! Chinner shouts out with a laugh and introduces us to each other.

Two best friends. Chinner and P.J. at Cosy Joe's 2019

* Barry McGuigan, born as Finbar Patrick McGuigan MBE (28.02.61 in Clones, County Monaghan) is an Irish retired professional boxer. McGuigan was nicknamed "The Clones Cyclone" and became a boxing world champion. He was very popular with Irish and British audiences, representing neutrality and peace in a time when Ireland, where he lived, was affected by The Troubles.

This is the first meeting of many for me and P.J. (Patrick), who is a long established friend of Chinner's. More pints. Lots of exchange of the most important facts. When did you come? How did you do? Pint?

P.J., I learn has been up the holy mountain Croagh Patrick altogether forty-three times. Ok, as a local man that might be a common thing to do. But when I first took the challenge to climb up this precious destination, I learned why there is so much more to it. P.J. took Chinner twice up to the top in the past and one time I learn they've both been under the influence…

Although I did not have the chance to climb up Croagh Patrick during our trip in May, I started to be fascinated with the challenge to do so.

P.J. really is a great character and I witness how much Chinner and him enjoy each other's company. When I got the Dictaphone out to keep some of P.J. stories on tape, he left this joke to us.

Paddy and Maggie were married. When he comes home from the pub, very little money left in the pocket. She tried all before, only give him 15 Euros and all sorts, she did counselling, nothing helps. Then someone suggested to Maggie, have a chat with your priest.

She tells him, I did the frying pan already!
Priest: You taking the wrong approach, why don't you kill him with kindness?

So when he comes in on a Friday, as always horrible drunk. With little left in the pockets, have a nice dinner for him there.
Candles on the table. Can of Guinness.
Ok, I give it a try, she says.

Comes Friday, Paddy comes home…
Ducks away from the frying pan as usual, no frying pan this time, instead an elaborate meal on the table.

"Candles? What's going on here?"

She says: "Patrick will you like to sit down at the top of the table?"

So he takes the chair, still waiting for this frying pan to come.

And he has the wonderful meal, and the meal is finished, she says, "Patrick maybe sit near the fire in your armchair and read the Mayo news", he still looks out for the frying pan, "and would you like another can of Guinness?"

"Oh I would love one of those!"

She is in the kitchen, the fire is getting low, and Guinness is gone.

She is on one side of the fire, he on the other, still ducking for the pan to come.

She says, "Patrick its half past nine, do you think we will go to bed?"

Then he says "if I go home now she will kill me altogether!"

Late afternoon we return to the base at Castle Court hotel and find some of the boys relaxing in the yard. Ivan looks like a happy bunny, wearing sunglasses and a navy commander cap he and Graham are having an obviously great time.

I join them for a while and as I suffer a bit from the very bright sun, Graham folds me a provisional hat from a hanky.

Graham: "Now he nearly looks like an Englishman!"

Going up to the room for a little refreshment I take a photo of an old oil painting showing the holy mountain Croagh Patrick which is so important for Westport. The style reminds me of my dad's artwork. He was a nature and landscape artist beside many other talents.

After another exciting day we're all bound to go for a special meal tonight at around eight o'clock. What a feast! I forgot where that was…

The people part 3

Steve Johnson was on the trip to Ireland last year. He got knowledge of the trip through his local, the Tiger pub. Last year some chaps dropped out, they were from the London area and Chinner asked Steve if he was interested, so he said yes.

Steve: "And I enjoyed it and came again".

Steve is now 65 years old. He comes originally from East London, left London in 2012, then lived in Broadwindsor in Dorset. After retirement he moved to Bridport and lives now at West Allington. That was two and a half years ago.

A professional slater and tiler he was, he likes to point out that there is a big difference between that and a roofer!

This trip he shares with J.D., who he knows already from his time at Broadwindsor as he lived there too. Been asked what he likes to tell the readers in particular, he has nothing in particular, but he likes to point out that he really enjoys the stay at Westport!

Mark Roe is 35 years old and born in Dublin.

He met his partner Nicola in Orlando / Florida, 2007, she was on holiday and so was he and they met in an Irish pub, called the Lucky Leprechaun. Nicola has lived already in Bridport for nearly 20 years and Mark joined in with her.
Mark is a trained as graphic designer and works today in Bridport as a net maker.

He knows Chinner, as he was married to Nicola's aunty and that's how he learned about the trip to Westport. He knew Charlie, as he calls Chinner, quite some time and they became friends and now it's the first time he joined in and he really enjoys it.

His mum Dorothy, his sister Dorothy and her partner Derrick with nephew Alan came to Westport during our stay from Dublin to meet up. It is only three and a half hours' drive from Dublin.

Mark calls himself a Dublin boy, living in Westbay, which is the harbour of Bridport.
He says it is a wonderful trip, some really nice people, nice to be back home in Ireland. All the hospitality and pubs. People are friendly here; they make you welcome, not many places in the world you get that. Scotland as well has similar hospitality.

Grant Connolly, born in New Zealand, in the town of Tauranga which is the biggest port of NZ. That's the North Island, about 120 miles south of Auckland. Grant came at the age of seven with his parents to England and is now 61 years old.
He lives in Burton Bradstock, near Bridport on the caravan site. I ask him, what you doing for a living? Ripping the grockles off is his answer (holidaymakers, especially those visiting a resort in Dorset, Devon or Cornwall). But really it is looking after the holiday makers, whom we say we hate, but without them Bridport would die and be a ghost town. We all know that.
"We sell them lodges, very posh caravans; they buy them and rent the pitch to friends as holiday cottages if not using them themselves."
I ask Grant I never saw any caravans near Burton. "No", he says, "You can't see the site from the road. Not like Westbay, bit more up market.

This is the third time Grant is on the trip to Westport, last year and the year before he joined in, and he says, it is good fun, good giggle, good bunch of boys, the core of same once, and new faces. When I ask him if he doesn't get bored to go to the same places again, he says: "No I like it, the valley with Ivan, Achill and all this! "My first year was at Dunning's, which was the last stay there, then we went over to the hotel on the other side of Castle Court but same complex."

Watching the racing is my hobby. I own nine motor bikes, cause I'm greedy, 'because I can, they not in cling film, five are runners, others just need tax or MOT. They all in nice nick, reasonable condition, but I don't do shiny.

Me: "Have you got a Harley Davidson?"

"No! Rubbish. My newest bike is fifteen years old. BSAs mostly, classics. I've got two modern ones. I like comfortable biking, cruising. Not proper sports bikes.

I go to the Isle of Man, most years,

Me: "Are you married?"

I have been. And it's wise, not going for the hat-trick.

Ivan turns up, Grant says, I get interrogated, I say, sorry we swapped places for an interview and Ivan asks, whose permission did you get?

Sunday, 19th of May

Turns out Robbie gets up first, suits me. We are a well organised room team. Comes my turn and after a long relaxing bath and big breakfast the group set off for another exploration. Ivan, Grant and I take the 007 car and head towards the Atlantic Way again.

Ivan gives directions and he obviously has got a plan. Grant drives highly efficiently as always and I try to catch some photos of the countryside flying past. Croagh Patrick! I shout to them in the front. No mercy for the reporter to slow down for photos or even have a halt. We leave the main road and turn right towards the Murrisk Abbey again.

Two hundred yards only and Ivan orders the car to stop and he refers to the famine memorial which is behind a row of trees and looks like the Flying Dutchman has landed in a cow field. As Ivan and Grant have seen this monument already several times before, they decide this time to stay by the car and I make my way on foot around the stranded boat.

The National Famine Monument was unveiled in 1997.

More than a million people died in Ireland from disease and starvation during the Great Famine of 1845 to 1849. In 1996 Murrisk was chosen as the appropriate site to erect a national monument. Renowned sculptor John Behan was commissioned by the Government to create a sculpture that would encompass the magnitude of the suffering and loss endured by the people of Ireland during the famine.

The result was the Famine Ship, a bronze memorial, with skeletal figures symbolizing the many people who died in the "Coffin Ships" that set sail from Ireland in desperate hope of escaping to a better life.

The famine memorial is in sight of the holy mountain and as it is again such a clear and sunny day, I can shoot a brilliant photo.

This special memorial is reminding us of the time when the potato famine took place. In 1845 a fungus began to destroy the potato crops, causing the green leaves to blight and rot. The whole of Ireland suffered a complete devastation. County Mayo was particularly struck hard, as nearly all of its population was dependent on the potato. Many died or left Ireland and County Mayo alone lost 100,000 people to death and emigration at that time.

Still not quite sure what this day's program looks like but, after we left the famine memorial, not much later we were again at Murrisk Abbey.

What is known to us as Murrisk Abbey was a Friary founded on lands granted by Thady O'Malley in 1457 to Hugh O'Malley of Banada Friary. Behind all this was the idea to bring faith to the inhabitants of this part of the county and establish a church and priory near Croagh Patrick, the holy mountain. History says it was built on the site which before had housed the original church founded by St. Patrick.

Ivan sits again all alone on the green bench. He positions himself right at the site and I can visualize who sits next to him in his mind and in the background the holy mountain is enthroned. I like that.

The tide is out today so my interest is focused on the 5th century abbey. What I find remarkable is that the doors are all very low. Even I can reach the top beam standing in it. Must be a special reason for that as I don't think people were that small in general then, or maybe yes?

Murrisk Abbey 5th century door heights

After a short stop over at the abbey, we drive on and follow the "Wild Atlantic Way" southwards. This is all part of what is called the "Bay Coast" which stretches from Keem Bay on Achill south past the town of Galway. Further south the "Wild Atlantic Way" becomes the "Cliff Coast". At Louisburgh we join the R378 and it is signposted towards the Carrowniskey Beach. We stop at a high point from where the view looks out to the Atlantic. Huge waves are coming in from the southwest, rolling on towards the shoreline which looks like a flock carpet. Rocks and small cliffs are changing to smaller stretches of beaches. We are a bit inland and the wind seems to stop at the bank. We enjoy another lovely sunny day with blue skies. Lots of sheep can be seen around here. They all graze freely and are marked with coloured dots by their owners.

Carrowniskey Beach or better Carrowniskey Strand is well known among wind surfers. The beach itself is just a very long stretch of fist size pebbles. But who needs fine sand when surfing? "Surfmayo", a company located in nearby Louisburgh has got an outlet just on the beach and they offer seven days a week surf lessons. www.surfmayo.com

The car park lies very close to the shoreline and we are one of the only three cars parked up today. One is a Gardaí patrol car and of course Ivan goes and has a chat with the men as he is himself a former Metropolitan copper. I join them after a while and learn from the police officer, that Drogheda, the town where I used to live for twelve months is today a dangerous place and a hot spot of drug related gang crime. How things can change. When I spent a lovely time there it seemed to be the most safe, happy place.

The Gardaí Síochána was formed in the year 1922 in Ireland as the police constabulary of the free Irish state. 1925 then the former Dublin Metropolitan Police was merged with it and became Garda as we know it today.

We continue our Sunday excursion and head up a lane which displays a signpost "Fishing for all" as Grant might be interested to give it a go some day. Unfortunately at the very end of the lane is nothing but a closed gate. Okay, reverse and further south we drive.

Another winding road with some sheep in the way at a bend and they really take their time to wander off. No traffic at all. Considering it is already towards the end of May, I rate that as a good sign. It means no mass tourism with all the nasty side effects.

A car park next to a beach is our destination. Just us here this time and Ivan seems to be kind of proud to have guided us here. He stays near the car this time. This is Silver Strand!

"Too far to walk" he claims and fifteen minutes later I realise what he was talking about. Grant and I make a relaxed stroll towards the see which looks like it is a half mile in the distance.

Ivan: "It's not the end of the world, but you can see it."

White flat sand under the feet. The mandatory sheep grazing the dunes. God knows how this animal managed to get on here. At the car park it's all fenced, and one has to walk through a gate, the sheep might have a key to that. One must have been caught by the incoming tide. I find some remains and my first thought was it's from some fish. But then I can spot the woolly sheepskin intertwined with bones and sand.

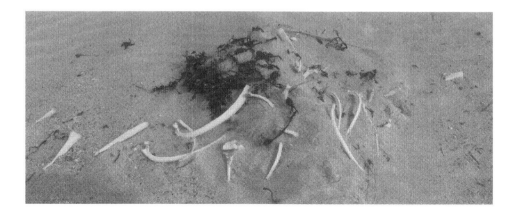

Grant turns to the left; southwards and he obviously know his way as he has been here before on previous trips. I head straight on towards the sounds of the rolling in sea and pass through fifteen foot of sand dunes which look immaculate healthy from an ecological point of view.

No footsteps of humans, just the sheep were here. The strong grass bends with the westerly winds. It reminds me very much of those dune nature reservoirs at the Baltic in the north east of Germany.

What a strand! Wish I could add for you here the bit of filming I took. The wind rustles alone and only a few birds calling sometimes. The waves rolling as long swell on the absolutely flat beach.

It's hard to leave a place like this. Ivan gave us thirty minutes, fair enough. But it will leave an ever lasting impression.

Some when early afternoon we are back at the hotel. J.D. sits comfortably inside the bar area and enjoys one of the house lunches and I decide to join and order just a sandwich for now. Later I try out the hotel computer and only to learn it is still there, but not functional anymore as the receptionist explains. I get told that today nearly everybody's got an iPhone and there is no demand anymore for this service. Glad I had some bites for lunch as we all meet up at half past four to celebrate the trips traditional G&T session. It all started way back when Graham once bought a variety of Gin at the airport and today, we meet up at his and Grant's temporary home, room number 3232. Slowly but steadily everybody arrives and beside Gin and Tonic we have some red wine too in case one doesn't like the spirits.

It gets nicely packed and Chinner and Mark carry some chairs over from their room. Some sit on the bed and Graham as the host with Robbie as his assistant prepare bowls with sliced up cheese, crisps, olives, nuts, crackers and all sorts of snacks that might go well with the Gin. Of course we got ice too! Cheers!

After a few enjoyable mixes Ivan switches the house music off and orders me to stand up in the middle and asks me to take the shirt off. Then I have to take a paper bag over the head and as it does not quite cover the view, I can see Ivan presenting me a tee shirt and as he takes the bag off he congratulates me as the chosen number one guy of this trip. Wow! I am gob-smacked. I received an original Matt Molloy's tee shirt to go with the nomination. I cannot tell you how proud I felt and slipped into this black shirt to have a toast on the role and touch glasses with everyone. If you ever come across Mark, he did a video of that event and has got it on his iPhone.

Time off and everybody has a bit of a rest before later we take a taxi minibus to carry us down to the harbour. Grant is missing and Chinner is concerned and rings him. Okay, he is just late, and we wait a bit. Chinner looks not only after the tour kitty but everyone. He cares a lot. Drives Ivan made (laughs out loud).

Tonight it's oysters and mussels with French fries, prawn cocktail and that sort of stuff. Reads very simple, sounds very simple but it will be outstanding and delicious! We attend the Towers Restaurant which is at the end of the pier down in the harbour housed in a blue painted semi-modern building decorated with flower baskets at the outside and this place is famous for the seafood.

Not that long ago Westport used to have a huge fishing industry. The boats were stationed at Westport harbour and there is even a giant fish factory next to the harbour, which is out of use today. What is left of these times is the popularity for fish restaurants and there is still fishing on a small local scale around Westport.

As we booked beforehand (okay, Ivan did) we are led by one of the waitresses to our table at the back of the premises in a kind of a conservatory. The restaurant looks pretty busy, but it does only take a very short time and we all have a first drink to start with and start studying the menu. As far as I remember all of us ordered some seafood. Starters like fishcake, fried sardines, prawns on salad in French dressing give us an idea what we can expect of the main dishes.

We ask as usual for a few bottles of red and white wine. Some stick to the Guinness and no water or coffee tonight as we are not driving. Everybody enjoys the stunning views over the bay into the Clew Bay with a sun downer out of a holiday brochure. And between starters and the main meal some of us go and stretch the legs outside on the green which ends right at the sea only separated by a stone wall. People sit out here; admire the scenery, some smoke, some do both. Ivan says, "I always take you to nice places". How right he is!

Clew Bay view from the "Tower Restaurant" with the holy mountain

Back at the table he tells us about his visit to the church today. He went to join the afternoon mass. Then he writes a message to the owner of the pub and passes it to the waitress. Just a friendly note that we are here again and do enjoy their food and service.

Chinner lets us know that he is ever so happy. Happier than ever in his life before. Okay, we know that's a bit overstated, but it describes very well how we all feel.

Monday, 20th of May

07.50 hours! This is rather early to wake for me. Slept very well again at the Castle Court and Robbie my roommate is already doing his morning rituals in the bathroom. I'm in need of a wee and he doesn't mind I join the bathroom as it is quite comfortable, and Robbie can close the bathtub curtains to stay private.

After breakfast having our very own waitress Veronica back and us sitting at tables specially arranged by her again, I start working on diary writing and see who I can catch for a short interrogation.

I learn a little bit about the previous trips and so far, I can confirm the crews were as followed:

Trip no. 1*
Ivan and Jay Jay

Trip no. 2*
Ivan, Irish Tom (Thomas McLaughlin), "Drunken" Duncan

Trip no. 3*
Ivan, Chinner, Irish Tom (Thomas McLaughlin), Weasel (Peter)

Trip no 4 - 2013
Ivan, Flash (Dave Gordon), Irish Tom (Thomas McLaughlin), Chinner, Dodge, Robbie, Paul (Heinzie), Terry, Mutter

Trip no. 5 - 2014
Ivan, Rafique, Chinner, Chris Lindsay, Paul

Trip no. 6 - 2015
Ivan, Rafique, Chinner, Alan Campbell, Robbie, Edward, Dodge, Tucky

Trip no. 7 -2016
Ivan, Rafique, Chinner, Alan Campbell, Tacky, Dodge, Robbie, Chris Lindsay, Graham

Our very good friend Dodge (Roger) died in September 2016. R.I.P. we will always remember you!

Dodge with Ivan at J.J. Finan

Trip no. 8 -2017
Ivan, Rafique, Chinner, Graham, Grant, Tacky (Nick Tuck), Snowy, Irish Paddy

Trip no. 9 - 2018
Ivan, Rafique, Chinner, Morty, Edward, Graham, Robbie, Grant, Steve

Trip no. 10 - 2019
Ivan, Chinner, Grant, Graham, J.D., Steve, Horst (that's me☺),
Robbie, Mark

And by looking at this list I must admit I do like the English
humour. They even laugh about death. Ivan said:" Dodge is the
only one who died. So far!"

* As there are no written records it was not possible to provide
the complete list of names from all trips. If you find yourself
missing here please come forward and it will be corrected with
the 2nd edition.

I sit out in the sun and bit by bit other members of this trip show
up. Grant and I separate for an interview with the "Dic" as they
call my smart little Dictaphone. Ivan joins our table and takes his
teeth out to stow them safely in his pocket. Ok, this way he can't
lose them as it happens sometimes and then Chinner is usually
the one who picks them up for him. J.D. didn't show up all
morning and the others blame him as a light weight, although
they claim he is Scottish and shouldn't be light weight, therefore.

I ask Graham if he can imagine such a trip the other way around.
Like men from Westport would travel to our hometown Bridport.
No way would they do that he says. "The Irish want to take the
money from the English"!

Then we do the interview with Grant and I learn new things
about motorbikes and New Zealand. You can find all in chapter
"The people part 3".

Later in the morning I decide to have a walk round town on my own to collect some local impressions. Take some photos and maybe catch some interesting people. As from July to September there are organised free walking tours explaining the history of Westport. At www.westportheritage.com one can find detailed information.

Today I cross the road on my own outside the hotel main entrance and walk down Distillery Road. I'm soon away from the vibrant town centre and pass some workmen houses, probably built in the 1950s. All looks quite simple here. Crossing the bridge over the Carrowbeg River which flows through the town I can spot some fish. Haven't seen any back in Bridport for quite some time, although we have three streams passing through town.

Opposite a place called Distillery Court I detect the very first Charity shop in Westport. And the winner is… Bridport as we have got six or seven or eight of them… says it all. This one has restricted opening times, only a few hours, three days a week. At the end of this road gathers a huge group of cyclists, maybe fifty of them. Later I learn that from here one can start off to cycle the route which makes a connection towards the harbour and from their one could continue the Atlantic Way passage. Or one takes the opposite direction which would lead towards the north and right up to Achill.

Continuing my walk on Altamont Road I notice a petrol station. The brand is named "Top", which reminds me to former East German ones. Diesel costs 1.37 € and unleaded you get for 1.49 € (Prices May 2019 and as I write this now a year later the gas prices have slumped worldwide, but I leave it here as it was). This one is active and in use of course unlike the one just outside the Castle Court. There you see three pumps in front of a building with its windows painted white and although it must be from the late 1950s one gets the impression this place was only abandoned three weeks ago. A bit of history conserved in the street view here.

Little bit further to the right is Castle Vets which looks rather like a Chinese herbal shop. Actually I haven't noticed many pets like in Bridport here so far. Guess two dogs, that's it. But here there is more Guinness around. Every pub has got this brand advertised as the priority. It is definitely Guinness land! I wonder if they would sponsor my book... we have to drink more, I guess.

A bit further out of town there is the WestPoint shopping centre. A Tesco supermarket, Boots pharmacy, Life Style Sports, Euro Giant, a small independent butcher called Walsh's, Carraig flower shop, Mr. Bananaman (forgot what that was) and a centre for the children named Wild West. At the other end of the huge free parking space sits the medical centre. All does not look overly busy on a Monday at noon.

Walking towards the old railway bridge I can spot some green grass which one won't find this bright anywhere in the world as on the emerald island. As I approach closer, I must laugh about myself being so easy tricked out by artificial green. But mind you, very well made! And the place looks tidy without any littering.

Next to the railway station which seems to be busy in operation is left the closed old Railway Tavern. The train station is the terminus station on the Dublin to Westport rail service. The line connects the town for passengers to or from nearby Galway. I spot a long train loaded high up with pine logs which is part of the local trade.

Further out of town on the left I learn where the Berlin people got the idea for their holocaust memorial from. There is a huge concrete plant which is producing all sorts of concrete products. In their yard they display the ready products spread out in the sun. It looks like it is not only Pharmacy industry and Tourism in Westport.

Going underneath the railway bridge unfortunately the footpath comes to an end and the road gets narrower. But I decide to keep on walking a little bit further to get a glimpse what Westport looks like from the outside. Pass the town boundary and on the town sign it says "Welcome to Westport" – Tidy town's national winner 2001, 2006, and 2008. I think it should get 2019 definitely too. It looks ever so clean over here. (Hey Bridport town here is something you could learn!) On the bottom of the sign is stated that Westport rated the best place to live in Ireland according to the Irish Times.

All over the place there is building activity. Mainly new houses, all detached, and I cannot see the common housing estates as we know in Bridport.

And there he is again. The holy mountain Croagh Patrick. Visible from all over the place. This time it produces the background of a farmer's battle with his sheep. I stop and watch him for twenty minutes how he tries to separate one animal from the flock to give it an injection. Oh Lord, it's just around midday but he must be drunk and so to his sheep dog. The attempts they undertake are better than any comedy you get presented on television. He gives his commands, whistles, shouts, swears, but the dog is manic and runs all over the place, making his efforts gained from a minute before disappearing. Good for him, and the sheep, after twenty minutes chase the injection gets done.

So many beautiful cottages around here. I can understand why this town is so popular to live in. Back on my way towards the centre there is this bungalow with a high metal fence all around and as I pass it, I find out the reason for that. It is the home of five huge Doberman dogs trying to get a piece of me.

Coming downhill the town looks ever so cozy spread out in front of me. I pass the Westport cycle and foot path which fits nicely into the suburb and is clearly marked with different coloured tarmac, one side for the bikes and the other for walkers. Walking down Shop Street towards the Octagon with the memorial column in the middle of the square I notice another Italian restaurant. Feels like I have already seen five of them since we arrived here and five Italian ice cafes too. They have names like "Il Volcano" or "La Bella Vita". To the left is the "West Coast Rare Books". One of six book shops counted so far.

Westport is not all and only about tourism. A huge employer is the pharmaceutical industry too. Allergan Pharmaceuticals Ireland is based in Westport since 1977 and the current facility, which is located at the Westport business park, only couple of hundred yards away from town center has grown to over 750,000 sq/ft on a 61 acre campus. The Westport Campus is a sterile pharmaceutical ophthalmic and biologics plant.

It is of great importance to the wider population in Westport, of which about 25% are employed by Allergan. They manufacture a range of branded medicines, such as Botox, therapeutic products and a wide range of treatments for eye diseases.

Another Westport company is named one of the best places to work. AMO, Abbott Medical Optics, got recognition being one of Ireland best workplaces. They're based at the same campus.

Maybe the tight connection with the pharmacy started a long time ago. In the town centre there is Treacy's Pharmacy. It says outside on the shop board: Nolans 1559-1994. Tom Treacy 1994.
I wonder if this place is the source which brought the today's pharma industry to Westport. I was told some 12,000 people find employment here.

Nolans 1559-1994. Tom Treacy 1994. Pharmacy in Westport

Turning back into the hotel's courtyard I find some of my friends enjoying the quiet place in lovely sunshine. Ivan for the first time without his standard blue jumper, he wears a white top and a Guinness cap. J.D is smartly dressed as always, and I notice his expensive leather shoes which he wears with green and white hooped socks. Perfect Irish colors! But then the white and blue checkered and perfect ironed shirt gives a bit of a contrast. His sunglasses are pushed above the forehead.

Grant with sunglasses and wears a New Zealand biker shirt together with a very visible necklace and the hat he covers his bold head with reminds me of Paul Hogan as Crocodile Dundee. With Chinner I notice his coloured arm braces made of little beads and his watch which has got an orange strap. His 1960s "Uncle Alfred style" zebra black and white hat you must see yourself by looking at the photo! It reminds me of this special type of camouflage painted on ships in WW1. I think the system is called dazzle camouflage. And there is Steve, reliable straight casually dressed as usual and wearing a blue tight shirt. I like it. Irish Mark, the youngest of the crew goes out with a pair of red short shorts today and it looks surreal as he walks through the door same time as the guy with the builder's arse as we called him. He entertained us a short while by exposing himself this way and insisting he is a millionaire hiding here for a secret holiday. Now you want to know what I was wearing, do you?

Everybody is relaxed and now I ask myself, did they wait for me? What's next?

I navigate first to my room and on the staircase at the second floor (I always take the stairs now!) I notice the two cats sunbathing on a corrugated roof. One is a tiger black and white and the other a black cat. Later I find out, the two lay there very often. At the room I can see the nearby graveyard for the first time from the window. Must go and inspect that place as exploring and photographing graveyards are my hobby for many years and I have done so all over the world.

Downtown cemetery

On the previous trip the group stayed at the other part of the hotel complex. It is under the same management but operates with a different name. It is called "Westport Plaza Hotel" and we would have stayed here again, but it was fully booked. The place looks a little bit more glamorous to me.

This evening dinner is planned at their restaurant. You can call it our steak night. Accompanied by lots of wine as usual and I must admit their selection is rather good!

After a satisfying meal and another pleasant evening spent with my fellow comrade traveler friends I decide on an early night. Back to the Castle Court where I watch a bit of telly, Irish politics and European weather, Berlin 17 degrees. Here it was really warm today. "Wenn Engel reisen", German proverb (when angels travel).

Tuesday, 21st of May

Bad hair day I guess is the right English expression. But after the bountiful breakfast life feels much better. It's supposed to be another "day off", means no fixed program for all of us. Only plan is to visit the Helm restaurant down at the harbour for our last evening in Westport this time and share a meal together.

I decide to do what tourists all over the world might do at some point and stroll downtown for a little shopping experience. I noticed the days before that Westport has a large variety of high quality shops offering anything one might need.

One shoe shop takes my attention and I decide on my next visit to Westport to replace my whole shoe fleet here. They offer a huge selection of footwear which one finds usual only in shopping malls over in Dubai, Hong Kong or Rome. Not only shoes but various other stylish leather products such as belts and even hats are for sale.

It feels a relief coming from Bridport and finding here that not every third shop is a cheap shop or charity outlet of some kind. Westport offers a selection of fashion, art, books and even the hardware store seems to be more up market. How do they do that?

The town looks busy and I notice the balance between cars and pedestrians is significant towards the foot folks. It only comes to your mind you might consider crossing a road and it feels like the drivers can read your thoughts and wave you over. Oh dear, back in Bridport this is so different. Even mothers with a baby stroller are targeted and as an elderly person there is hardly any chance to cross the road and not become a victim of road rage. Ok, rant over.

Chinner rings just to check if I am okay as he hasn't seen me the morning. Good man. Everybody needs a Chinner!

The taxis operating over here are all minibuses. They use mainly eight seaters and I haven't seen any car cabs so far. My favorite Westport taxi to recommend as a former taxi driver from Bridport would be "T.J CABS" on 087-7439 600. The driver contributed lots of information, as cabbies do.

There are at least eight bike hire stations all over the town. Cycling seems to be very popular. Looks like the right approach for a modern community to handle the local traffic and offer something practical, affordable and fun for the tourists to explore the place.

The plan is to set off at 6.30 pm for today's dinner. The taxi is ordered which will bring us down to the harbour and this time we visit "The Helm". It's the oar!

As everybody slowly assembles in the courtyard, I take my time and walk through the back of the hotel and have a quick look at a graveyard. They are really next to each other. I think: "First hotel with private memorial park"!

Minibus today is only for eight passengers, so one has to sit in the boot behind the back seats. Chinner volunteers for that and the driver is happy for him to do so.

Mark lets me know that he stayed at "The Helm" two years ago together with his mother and sister, the kids and his partner. Very nice place he promises.

And by now this is nothing new to me. The menu is so inviting and tasty it makes any decision to order a very difficult task.

We place an order which probably challenges every waitress as everybody has his very own choice and to get it all right the young lady calls her collogue to assist. Two French onion soups. Oh let's start here. Two bottles of wine, they call it simply red and white. She is happy to take our orders for the bar too and we order another four pints of Guinness, Gin & Tonic, yes with ice and lemon and please one coffee. Who is that?

THE HELM

Homemade Soup Of The Day
French Onion Soup
With Croutons & Grated Parmesan Cheese
Helm Seafood Chowder
Breaded Mushrooms
Stuffed With Cream Cheese & Garlic
Crown Of Melon
With Fresh Fruit
Kelly's Black Pudding
Served On A Bed Of Mash Potato With Scallion
& Balsamic Dressing
Clew Bay Mussels
Steamed In White Wine & Lemon Butter
Deep Fried Prawns
Breaded King Prawns With A Sweet Chilli Dip
Fresh Crab Meat
With Marie Rose Sauce & Side Salad
Fresh Crab Claws
Tossed In Garlic Butter
Deep Fried Brie
With Cumberland Sauce
Duck Spring Rolls
With A Sweet Chilli Dip
Fresh Prawn Cocktail
With Marie Rose
Fresh Clew Bay Scollops
With Kelly's Black Pudding
Served With A Lemon & Leek Sauce
Notice- should you b

The Helm special seafood chowder; fresh crab claws tossed in garlic butter, deep fried brie with Cumberland sauce; roast rack of lamb with rosemary thyme and jus; one prime sirloin of beef cooked to your liking, in this case medium, served with sauté onions and sauces; Clew Bay mussels, steamed in white wine and lemon butter…

After the starters we join the bar between courses to have another drink and soon the main courses are dished up. Wow! The tables seem to be too small for all that. What a feast.

Before we start eating one has to place a few beer mats under one leg of the table as it is all over the world, restaurant tables can be wobbly sometimes.

Chinner goes for the Panko breaded calamari with curry mustard dip, side salad and chips. I decide to try the breaded monkfish tail scampi with a tartare sauce and as my chips arrive later so Chinner offers me to share his first. The red wine goes well with that scampi.

Roast rack of lamb with rosemary thyme & jus, my favorite!

Fillets of John Dory with a lemon and herb sauce are served and one goes for half a lobster with garlic butter and peppercorn sauce. After this spoiling there comes a storm of mobile texting to transfer the view of the food to the beloved ones at home. That has to be shared!

Table 21, 21st of May, 321.50 €, How good is that, the happy number 21? I think it was wonderful. That includes the wine and we are more than happy to leave a generous gratuity.

As our jolly trip to Westport nearly comes to an end, we talk a lot tonight about it and share our views and news. As it is, everything is always a matter of opinion and semantically a dead fish is not always something to eat. Back later in the hotel I find Ivan sitting on his own at the bar and I guess he thinks... probably of old times and that he is very proud to bring us here. I do hope so. Each night there is some function in the bar and tonight they have a music duo. Father and daughter, playing together for forty years according to their little poster next to the speakers. They're named "Family Affairs", of course and play country western music. This again suits the crowd in the bar, mainly Americans tonight as there arrived a new load today. I must explain here that the Castle Court Hotel is very famous for traveler groups from the United States and they give the place a steady flow of customers.

And it just happens that Grant and Chinner join me and we enjoy watching the people and listening to the music. The old folks, mind you 99% women, besiege the dance floor. The men look rather dead (sorry men) and watch the goings on there from a safe distance at the tables. There is a tiny taste of Alzheimer here tonight. Bless them. Grant wears an Aston Martin racing shirt and drinks Lager. Chinner is on the Guinness and I come back from the bar with my latest discovery. I chatted to two guys from Dublin and they introduced me to a Port and Brandy drink which can become my future favorite now. I do a bit of dancing and as I accompany the dear lady back to her table the husband who is defiantly over ninety nearly starts a fight. He is jealous. Later I learn he has Alzheimer's and has just been seventy years back in time in his mind. After the second dance he reacts friendly and happy when his lady returns. Walking back to my room along these corridors it all reminds me of my time serving on a passenger liner in the Caribbean. The American tourists, the alleyways with all the cabins and the slight lurches and rolling under my feet.

That was another good day!

Wednesday, 22nd of May

The last morning to wake up at Castle Court hotel and I discover there is still a Bible in the drawer next to my bed. Some hotels don't do that anymore due to political correctness. But here we are in Ireland, a traditional strict Catholic society. Okay, not that I would start reading it now, just thought to mention it. It reminds me what Helen, that's the wife of the boss whose trucker company handled our pipelines those days in Drogheda, told me. I had asked her why it seems to be quite complicated to date over here and her reply was: "The girls know you are leaving after a year and they want to get married as they are Catholic". Makes sense.

Last breakfast and say goodbye to the toast machine. And of course farewell to our personal waitress Veronica who really looked after all of us so well. I must admit, the Castle Court Hotel was all over a very pleasant experience. Although quite a big house, this place is family run and one can feel it each day, they look after the guests and that's why the hotel has a reputation as a home away from home.

"Alles hat ein Ende. Nur die Wurst hat zwei!" (German proverb) which translates "Everything has an end. Only the sausage has two!" I must admit I have a split feeling. On the one hand I am somewhat surprised this lovely trip is already over, that's gone quick and at the same time it feels we have been here since forever. Guess both feelings express how much I enjoyed the stay. Today Ivan required an early start as we like to visit a few places of interest on the way to the airport for the return flight. 9.30 am is the time to meet up in the courtyard and today I am on time, finding J.D. sitting already in the morning sun.

But then only Ivan, Grant, Mark and I join the 007 car and leave at ten. The arrangements were that the others set off an hour later as they have already been where Ivan wants to take Mark and me for the first time.

Check out at the reception. Luggage stored nicely in the boot and Grant turns the 007 into the main road towards Knock on the N5. Not much traffic and Grant is a very good chauffeur which makes it pleasant to travel. After three quarters of an hour or so Ivan shouts, "take the next right" and Grant does so. We are in the countryside even more now as the N5 wasn't really a motorway with so little traffic. I still have no idea where Ivan wants to take us this morning. One turn right follows the next left one. Hedges line the country lanes and all you can see is what is in front of you. Our aim is a small hamlet near the town of Ballaghaderreen.

"Take a right turn at this farm on the right hand side of the lane and next left" Ivan instructs Grant and we approach another farmhouse bordering close to the lane.

This is Ivan's mum's birthplace. In April 1918 she arrived in the world in this remote part of the emerald island. And it goes even further back as her father was born at this farm too. Of course this provides a special moment again for Ivan and we are happy to share this with him and learn a little bit about how life has been here many years back.

Just opposite the farm hides one detached cottage overgrown by trees and shrubs. From over the road it looks rather abandoned. Only the front door is kept clear and shows that someone must go in and out here. As I approach it I can detect three motor bikes in which what used to be the drive. Mind you, the bikes blended perfectly with the building. One had the back wheel missing and all three looked a bit rusty. Further down another one. Looks like an early version of a Harley Davidson to me. Okay, the seat is missing here.

All together I counted twelve motorcycles and one sidecar. And just as I decided to enter the premises for further investigation a good sound of some rockabilly music starts playing. Obviously, someone was watching us. Small disappointment for Grant who loves bikes and for me just being curious in that kind of places.

"Come on boys, back in the car", Ivan calls over the road and we drive on. Not long after Ivan says something like "feck"! We got lost. "Turn back at the junction here and take the left instead". No, that doesn't look right either! To sustain Ivan's reputation as a local path finder I must admit there aren't any street signs, street or village names and naturally things change especially in the countryside where nature puts the biggest landmarks and changes the view every season. Finally we ask some road workers who luckily appear out of nowhere. My thought, yeah, usually workmen come from some fifty miles away these days, but not in Ireland! They are men from the local council. Ivan gets full instructions and after a few minutes we park up outside a small cemetery. It is the new graveyard of Tibohine and the last resting place of some of Ivan's ancestors and family members.

Just a couple of hundred yards further we stop at a proper sized countryside church. This church was built in 1858 only, but the history goes back as far as the 6th century and it was St. Patrick who inspired the people to have a first church at what is called Tibohine today.

St. Baoithin's Roman Catholic Church at Tibohine

We brought some white and yellow marguerites with us and next to the church we find the family graves of the Beinrne's where we lay them down. A lovely peaceful thing to do in the morning and the place spreads a nice and calm atmosphere.

Time to move on and we head towards the town of Ballaghaderreen which is just a kilometer off the N5 and only fifteen minutes' drive back to the airport. We've still got plenty of time before boarding our plane back home. The town basically assembles around the marketplace in the center and we easily find somewhere to park and just over the road is "Durkin's bar".

As we walk in, we are welcomed by the leggy waitress and sit down at a table next to the window. Ivan explains that this is the place where they usually meet up with some of his cousins who live in the area but today nothing had been arranged.

Two builders fortify themselves at the bar with full Irish breakfasts and a moment later I learn why they haven't got a pint of Guinness with it. No alcohol is served before twelve noon. Bugger! We take coffee and soft drinks instead. Mark, who joins a bit later walks in and asks straight what we are having, "Guinness, pint of…"? Sorry, no alcohol before twelve.

I decide on a walk round the square. Next to Durkin's bar is a local shop and the window display reminds me instantly of one I saw in former East Berlin in 1977. I share both pictures with you here. All gives an impression of simple and basic life conditions round here. Very much different from what I saw in Westport.

Fruit and veg outside shop at Ballaghaderreen

Fruit and veg in a shop former East Berlin 1977

The bar next door fits perfectly into this observation. It is called "The Hatch" on Main Street / The Square and has got a famous reputation regarding the Irish attempts to fight occupation by the British and in connection with the IRA. I was told that in that bar the IRA had conspiratorial meetings and it's related to a bombing which aimed at the British infantry barracks in those days in 1920.

Not long after one o'clock we circle into Knock airport rental car drop off point. Quick check around our 007 vehicle by a friendly and proficient lady, Grant pics up the paperwork and we stroll over the tarmac to departures. Taking a lift with our trolleys and shortly later we settle in the lounge on the first floor.

Still two hours until boarding and we use the time to have some food, which is of good quality. Chinner decides on a little nap on one of the many comfy benches, I explore a display which gives the details how Knock airport was founded and built as well as interesting facts about flying and planes in general. This airport is a five star one among the many I have travelled from. Not too busy and hectic, well organised and supplies all you need to cut two hours waiting time short.

Everyone has to pay ten Euro special airport fee towards the up keeping. Then a little hiccup with our administration as we find out that Grant's boarding pass print is the same as the incoming flight and he has to buy a new one for twenty €. I ask another passenger to take a photo of me wearing our martial arts tee shirt as we have a height competition running and Knock is 202 meters above sea level.

The area of Knock seems to have some magic to include. Nearby is the Knock Shrine, a unique pilgrimage destination. It's said that in 1879 fifteen people witnessed an apparition at the gable wall of the parish church. On giving their testimonies, the witnesses described a heavenly vision of Our Lady, St. Joseph, St. John the Evangelist and a lamb on an altar surrounded by angels. The angels were flying…

After a while we pass through boarding check and can enjoy a last drink in the lounge before leaving the emerald island for the time being. Everybody seems to be very happy with the outcome of our perfect trip to Westport and as I click the seat belt on the plane, I know I will come back pretty soon!

The total money raised for an unnamed charity was 36.00 €. That splits up among us as following: Ivan 2, Graham 11, myself 9 (how did that happen?), J.D. 2, Chinner 6, Grant 3, Mark 3, Steve 1 and Robbie nothing at all! During the trip we had three banned words and agreed if someone fails and mention "the war", BREXIT or work, the fine of one Euro is due.

And as a former platinum card holder of three international airlines I learned on the return flight to Bristol that Ryanair actually offers cheaper tariffs for swimmers, so they can have fewer life vests on board the plane. Clever Irish bastards!

Conclusion

It is absolutely possible to travel with a group of nice men for a week or so.

If you speak some English, the Irish will understand what you're after.

There is no need for vaccination when entering Westport (Ask you GP before you travel, just in case)

For a week you should calculate enough money to spend on drinks and the plenty of good food (Most attractions are free and there's live music in the pubs anyway). I would say Westport is less expensive than Bridport.

Not sure about visa and so on for English people after Brexit. Better check.

The weather is always very good. Best season for travel is January to December.

When over there and you run out of ideas what to do, you always can repeat the day before.

Knock airport is excellent to use. So is Bristol!

Driving in Ireland is on the right site. Or was it the left? I forgot. Anyway they measure in kilometers rather than miles.

It is absolutely safe in Westport. No crime spotted; friendly crowds and most importantly defensive drivers on the road.

Westport tourist office is highly recommended. But you would find the pubs and eateries on your own.

Useful addresses

National Tourism Development Authority
Discover Ireland Centre
Bridge Street
Westport F28 NF77
Co Mayo
T: +353 (0) 98 25711

www.wildatlanticway.com

JJ Finan's Bar & Lounge

Bar & Furniture & Hardware Shop & Off-license
Charlestown
https://charlestown.ie/business/jj-finans-bar-lounge/

Matt Molloy's / Westport
http://www.mattmolloy.com/

Achill tourist information
https://achilltourism.com/

Castlecourt Hotel / Westport
https://www.castlecourthotel.ie/

The Helm / Bar, restaurant, B&B and self catering
accommodation / Westport
https://www.thehelm.ie/

---

www.surfmayo.com

---

www.westportheritage.com

Barry McGuigan
https://www.google.com/search?q=Barry+McGuigan&rlz=1C1CHBD
_en-
GBGB800GB800&source=lnms&tbm=isch&sa=X&ved=2ahUKEwis2f
CSnpDpAhUOTRUIHd3oDw8Q_AUoAXoECBYQAw&biw=1920&bi
h=937

Some general information

Irish (Gaelic!) and English are the official languages.

Street and road signs are bilingual.

Smoking is not allowed in public areas.

St. Patrick's Day is on the 19th of March. Very important to know!

Road distances are in kilometers, but driving is on the left.

(They tried to change that to right side driving once and started the first week with lorries only. It didn't work!)

You can reach Ireland very easily with many airlines and there are regular ferry connections from the UK as well as from other parts of Europe.

Ireland has got the Euro (€) as currency. To change money is no problem whatsoever. The rate of conversion is as usual when travelling internationally, different depending where you change the money. My experience >

£ 100 in Bridport = 98.22 € (Travel agency)
100 € in Westport = £ 89.14 (Cash point)

By the way, the whole journey cost me about £ 900 and I heard from my friends, they spent about the same.

Huge range of high quality accommodation is available in and near Westport. Whether you fancy a break for a shopping tour and a pampering spa experience, a family holiday complete with children's club, or a personal apartment, this place provides it all. They have accommodation to suit every personality and pocket.

I personally recommend the "Castlecourt Hotel" in Westport and the "Helm" at the harbour to stay. The Helm provides self-catering rooms and cottages too. All top quality.

Westport is easily accessible via road or rail and is also just forty minute drive from Ireland West Airport, Knock.

No! It doesn't always rain in Ireland. We had the most sunny stay on our trip and from my previous time in the country I can tell, you might face all four seasons in day.

Printed in Poland
by Amazon Fulfillment
Poland Sp. z o.o., Wrocław